SHADOW MANOR

CANDACE NOLA

UNCOMFORTABLY DARK HORROR

Cover Art for digital, paperback, and hardcover editions by Christy Aldridge of Grim Poppy Design.

Edited and formatted by 360 Editing (a division of Uncomfortably Dark Horror).

Editor: Candace Nola.

Follow Uncomfortably Dark Horror for the best in indie horror reviews, author interviews and more. We are the exclusive publisher of the Dark Dozen Anthology series and the limited-edition hardcovers in 'dark' mode are only available on our website at www.uncomfortably dark.com.

PRAISE FOR SHADOW MANOR

"Shadow Manor is a lyrical gothic horror novella that engages the reader's senses from the very first page. Nola's way with words is as beautiful as it is haunting, captivating in ways that cleave, that tease, that endear. The mix of fear and intrigue found within these pages is intoxicating and even as one realizes they are unnerved, that they are frightened of what the next words might conjure, they are loath to look away."—L. Marie Wood, author of THE REALM TRILOGY and THE

PROMISE KEEPER.

"Nola's ability to tell a story is unmatched. Each book proves she is well on her way to becoming a legend." — Kristopher Rufty, author of OLD SCRATCH.

"Candace Nola has given us atmosphere, tension, and emotion before. Everything she produces is finely tuned and affecting, but Shadow Manor is her best yet. Whatever she has delivered in the past, she is bringing back to the table tenfold in this quiet, atmospheric, and hauntingly beautiful tale. She has such command over the quiet trepidation of being alone in the titular house that you don't even feel like you are reading a book... You're there in the Manor with Sinclair, and Nola has a vice grip on your heart as you follow Sinclair's descent into the dark secrets held within the house." - Megan Stockton, author of LOVELY, DARK, AND DEEP

"Candace Nola seems to re-invent herself with each passing book release. With

Shadow Manor, she takes us on a gothic journey that is equal parts harrowing and heartbreaking. In short, it is a must re ad."—John Watson, author of KARAOKE NIGHT.

"Candace Nola's Shadow Manor is a modern gothic tale of secrets, betrayal and misery. Brimming with delightfully icky prose, this heartbreaking haunted house tale sticks with you long after the last pag e."—Wendy Dalrymple, author of WHITE IBIS and ROSER PARK.

"Candace Nola brings the shivers, making the shadows come to life in this cobweb-covered treasure trove of buried secrets and macabre mysteries. I love a good ghost story, and Shadow Manor is a damn fine example."— Brennan LaFaro, author of the SLATTERY FALLS trilogy

"Candace Nola delivers a spine-chilling gothic tale reminiscent of Daphne Du Maurier's "The House on the Strand" but with more shocking twists and horrific

revelations. A young girl discovers the terrible events that occurred decades ago in an abandoned manor she shelters in during a storm. What happened in that house, and who is revealing its dark secrets? Find out in this chilling tale written by one of the best storytellers of our generation." — Jill Girardi, Co-author of WE'RE NOT OURSELVES TODAY (With Lydia Prime)

"In Shadow Manor, Candace Nola has shown she is a master of the macabre. This is a contemporary take on the gothic horror story—an isolated young woman trapped in a creepy mansion during a thunderstorm—and Nola builds up the tension mercilessly from the first page. If you want claustrophobia, shivers and an entertaining story to justify your fear of the dark, this book provides all that and so much more. This is a story that has echoes of The Ring, Fall of the House of Usher and so many other deliciously chilling stories that have kept me awake through the night. I cannot recommend this title enough: it's a definite must read."—Ashley Lister, author of CONVERSATIONS WITH DEAD SERIAL KILLERS

CONTENTS

DEDICATION

To the usual suspects: the kitty, the puddin', and the
sir.
For Mom.

For the Unicorn.

CHAPTER ONE

It was dark that night, blacker than tar, not a star in the sky. An eerie stillness leant tension to the humid air while shadows stretched skeletal fingers out across dim puddles of streetlight, only to be swallowed up by blackness once more. I had been walking for hours and a thunderstorm was swiftly approaching from the west. As heat lightning split the sky, a giant shadow loomed over me, suddenly appearing out of nowhere. Gasping and startled, I quickly began stepping backwards before I realized what it was. A giant house stood in front of me, just yards from where I stood.

I had been walking alongside a stretch of thick forest for so long, so deeply lost in my thoughts that I hadn't noticed when the trees thinned, and a stretch of lawn appeared. The wrought-iron fence beside me suddenly made clear as the lightning flashed again. I glanced up at the massive structure, trying to glean what I could from the lightning flashes.

It was a decrepit old girl. Once, a beautiful Victorian lady, now a dowdy old spinster fraught with age and rot. The wraparound porch, thick with green ivy and vines, sagged in places while other spots were rotted clean through. The windows were boarded up on the first level, but glass still glinted in the windows of the upper levels. The turrets stood tall, topped with gothic spires and gargoyles standing guard. The old house had a severe countenance to it, as if joy and laughter were forbidden here.

I reached the gate while I walked slowly ahead, staring at the house in hopeful trepidation. Pale stones lined the path to the massive porch where the heavily carved oak doors stood fast, an ornate brass knocker still fastened to each.

Standing at the gate, I debated, anxiously looking around at the still deserted street. I hadn't seen another person, house or car for over an hour, and a nasty storm was just about to start as I stood deliberating. Taking a deep breath, I lifted the latch for the gate and hurried down the pathway to the rickety porch just as the first drops of rain pelted the ground, hard and fast.

Cautiously, I went up the steps to the porch, hoping the wood was still strong. Well- placed steps guided me to the front door. Turning the knob, the heavy door groaned open. The sound sent a shiver racing down my spine. Stale air wafted from the house, assaulting my nose with mold, rot, and decay. One last look around told me what I already knew, not a car or person in sight; help was not coming, not tonight.

RESOLVED TO MY FATE, I pushed the door further open and stepped into the dark foyer. Wind rushed past me into the house, bringing a few stray leaves with it. Leaving the door ajar, hoping to get rid of the foulness in the air, I took a few steps towards the grand staircase and dug in my pocket for my cell phone. Pulling it out, I unlocked the screen and tapped the button for the flashlight app, turning it up as high as I could.

My feet and the floor were immediately bathed in a pool of light, and my body instantly relaxed. I hadn't realized how tense I had become as I exhaled in relief. Lifting the phone higher, I began to point it around me, looking at the house which I had taken refuge in.

"Hello?" I called out as I stood in the entryway. "Hellloooo, is anyone up there? I need some help, please. I'm stranded out here." I waited, listening for any sound, but none came.

Try again, Sinclair, I thought to myself. God forbid I find myself trapped with a bunch of squatters overnight. Best give them time to answer or make a noise so I could high-tail it out of there. I called out again, waited, but heard nothing. I sighed and looked around.

The foyer was massive, with the staircase right in front of me, a dark hallway leading deeper into the house, and large rooms laid out on either side. I assumed those were most likely the living and dining room. The floor looked like marble, as did the staircase. The windows were all intact, the boards only covered the outsides. Ornate stained-glass windows set into high arches over each door.

The room closest to me on the right was still partially furnished. A behemoth of a table was the focal point of the room and the light glinted off of it, like it was made of stone. A chandelier hung over it, dripping with beaded crystals. An enormous stone fireplace sat in the back corner of the room, flanked by a pair of ancient leather armchairs. Dining chairs were lined neatly around the table. A thick layer of dust coated everything, and cobwebs dripped from the chandelier.

As I wandered down towards the fireplace, I noted the wall of windows on my right, all boarded, but it must have been an impressive display when the house was inhabited. A carved buffet as long as the table sat beneath the windows. French doors closed the room off from the next, and an archway set into the left wall led into another hall.

A deafening clap of thunder sounded overhead, and I nearly jumped out of my shoes as my hand went up to my mouth to stifle a scream. Several seconds passed before my heart rate slowed and I let out a sheepish chuckle, laughing at my jumpiness. I had been so engrossed in my investigation of the house that I had almost forgotten the storm raging outside.

I remembered that I had left the front doors open and decided to close them before someone noticed, if anyone were to notice. I also didn't want any wildlife wandering into the house either and scaring the hell out of me. Taking one final look around the room, I began walking towards the foyer.

Shining the light from my phone around as I walked, I was further impressed by the details that had been put into the house. The doorways were heavily carved, as was the banister of the staircase. Marble statues were mounted above the stained-glass windows. These were smaller, but more grotesque versions of the gargoyles that sat atop the house, staring down at me with furious disapproval as I passed by the ornate windows.

Reaching the door, I pushed it closed against the wind and the rain, sealing myself inside the dark house. I stood there for several long minutes, back against the door, arms hanging limply at my sides, and just breathed. I was safe, for now, and could figure out my next steps. The house was old and creepy, but seemed solid enough to withstand the storm raging outside. It would do for the night, and at least I would be dry.

As ANOTHER CLAP OF thunder shook the windows, I pushed myself off the door and wiped a stray tear from my cheek. Now was not the time for tears. There would be plenty of time for that later. Right now, I needed to finish checking out my chosen refuge and see where I could camp out for the night. Tapping the light on my phone again, I pointed it up at the staircase and marveled in fascination at the enormous chandelier that hung two stories above the foyer.

Letting out a low whistle, I stepped forward a few steps. Standing directly under it, I let the light play off the glistening beads and crystals that still shone brightly under its layers of dust. I couldn't even begin to comprehend what it might have cost or how heavy it was. The last time I had laid eyes on a chandelier that big was at the city opera house on a school field trip.

Despite the eerie vibe of the house, I was anxious to see the rest of it. After being on the road for so long, it was a welcome respite. I have loved Victorian houses since my childhood. They made the most beautiful dollhouses, of which I had owned several. The high ceilings, the grand staircases, the turrets, and high spires, the gothic feel of them, their beauty was simply unmatched by other architecture.

I turned my light and my attention towards the other room that flanked the foyer and began walking towards it, fully expecting a formal living room. The shadowy hallway just behind me seemed to stretch on for miles, tempting me to shine my light into its depths, but I knew I would get there soon enough.

As I stepped through the doorway, I smiled slowly, already falling in love with the room. Bookcases lined the walls, built in under the front windows and on either side of the giant fireplace. Several musty chaises sat about the room, along with a half dozen elegant wingback chairs and a long, hand-carved sofa.

Sheet-covered antique tables sat next to the chairs and the sofa. Almost all were piled with books. An old baby grand piano sat in the corner opposite the fireplace and a large desk occupied the other corner, closest to the doorway.

More books, papers, and journals filled most of the shelves, alongside various figurines, Knick-knacks and several ship-in-a-bottle displays. Dust covered every surface, and cobwebs dripped from the various lamps and window frames. I wandered slowly about the room, almost reverently. This was the library of the home, the heart of any well-respecting Victorian lady, the showpiece of the era. In its heyday, this room would have been the most used for music lessons, studying, reading to pass the time, concerts for guests and general household affairs.

I knew I would find ledgers on the desk somewhere detailing household bills and other accounts, just like

I knew that the books on the shelves would be a wide range of subjects suitable for teaching and for reading. Reaching the piano, I ran my finger down several keys, listening in amazement to the notes as they struck, mostly still in tune. Dust mites swirled into the air as I struck a few more keys in delight.

Thunder shook the glass once more as the final notes faded away. I chuckled softly, shaking my head as I continued to shine my light across books and shelves. This would be where I would pass my time tonight. Curled up on an old chaise, reading a classic or two. I could already smell the musty scent of old parchment and ink, and my smile grew a bit wider. Inside, an errant thought flashed in my mind like neon, but then vanished just as quickly.

Why hadn't these things been packed? Why had the owners left so much?

THE THOUGHT DID LITTLE to raise any warning flags in my exhausted brain as I continued my perusal of the house. The storm raged outside; the wind battering the sides of the house as thunder rolled across the violent sky. Thick clouds blotted out any hope for stars tonight, and the moon didn't dare show her face. I left the library and wandered down the hall that led to the back of the home, discovering several more doors as I went. A parlor sat just behind the library, with a charming breakfast room and atrium situated behind that, in the left rear corner of the house. The hall itself led directly into the kitchen that ran along the back of the house, with a pantry on the right side.

The kitchen was huge, with double sinks along the rear windows facing the outside, an enormous old stove, from the early fifties, and a giant oak island in the middle, complete with a knife block, a hanging rack suspended over it and butcher block top. Cabinets and shelves lined the other walls, and a set of doors led out into the dining room that I had explored earlier.

The kitchen was much the same as the library, with dishes and cookware still nearly in its place. Old, canned goods still were tucked away in the cabinets, along with packets of tea, sugar, and the like. There was a door that led out onto a covered porch and from there into the yard, but it was secured with a deadbolt and a chain on the inside. More boards covered the glass windows on the porch as well as the storm door that led to the yard.

I shook my head and turned to go back down the hallway, curious as to what the other doors were that were tucked into the right side of the hall. I snorted quietly, mildly amused by my ridiculous curiosity. The doors probably hid normal things, like a closet or a washroom, perhaps a basement door. But I didn't care. I wanted to see it, anyway; I was fascinated. It wasn't like I was going anywhere for a few hours.

I paused at the first door and opened it, shining my phone around for a quick look. Just a simple powder room, elegantly decorated with a beautiful carved mirror over the vanity and several framed paintings on the opposite wall. Peach or maybe faded pink hand towels still hung limply on the towel rack. More cobwebs dripped from the corners and several spiders scurried away from my light.

Shuddering, I quickly pulled the door closed and walked the few steps to the next door. Just a deep closet that reached behind the staircase. Shelves lined both sides, holding cleaning supplies, rags, linens, light bulbs and an old canister vacuum cleaner. A wry smile covered my face when I saw it. My mom had one when I was a child, and I've never used a better vacuum than that old Electrolux. I pulled the door closed and made my way back to the foyer and the grand staircase. I shone my light up the staircase one last time, seeing no real reason to go up there other than my own curiosity. I decided against it and turned to the library to settle in for the night.

Plopping down on the settee closest to the fireplace, I shrugged my backpack off and opened it on my lap, rummaging around for a lighter, hoping that I still had one in there. Not a smoker, but having a few friends that were, I invariably found myself collecting lighters along the way. Feeling a hard lump near the bottom lining, I dug down into the side pocket and grinned when I pulled the small neon tube from my pack.

I bounced back up on my feet, anxious to find a candle or two, and cringed suddenly when thunder shook the house again. My heart thudded hard against my chest as I looked on nearby shelves and tables for a candle. I found several candlesticks in the desk drawer and set them in an old pen holder that was on the desk and lit them, happy to have a bit of light other than my phone. I really wanted to save my battery so I could call my mom.

CHAPTER TWO

I KNEW SHE WOULD be worried. She warned me about Perry, but I didn't listen. I never listened, and here I was stranded, ten miles from home at least, in an abandoned house. She had never liked him, but I was too hung up on his good looks and popular status at school. I was eager for our date, determined to become his official girlfriend by the end of it. Sadly, our day at the beach had gone wrong when he began drinking and groping me in front of his friends, pushing for more than I wanted. I insisted he take me home. He got pissed and ended up dragging me out of his car halfway there, calling me a tease and an ungrateful bitch before speeding off into the night.

My pride was more hurt than anything, but I fully expected he would come back in a few minutes, realizing what an ass he was being, so I trudged along the roadside, not bothering to call for help. But those minutes had turned into hours. Perry had really left me and the understanding that I was to be only a piece of ass for him crushed me more than the abandonment.

I wasn't eager to tell my mom that she had been right once again, but I knew the moment I saw her, the whole story would fall from my lips in a torrent of tears and anger and hurt. I wiped a tear away, refusing to give in to my frustration and fear, and looked around the room again, grateful that I found this place just as the rain started.

It really was a beautiful old house, and I would have loved to have seen it when people lived here. The library was elegant and screamed of old money. The wood was hand-carved, shelves of ebony and mahogany, the fireplace built by hand, each stone set carefully in place. The books looked rich and hand selected, leather bound and hand–stitched tomes that smelled of parchment and ancient ink. Even the settee I sat on was covered in damask and woven through with opulent gold thread.

With a deep sigh, I tapped "Home" on my contacts list and waited for my mom to pick up. Several rings and a long minute later, I disconnected the call. She was probably busy doing laundry or was driving some place. I knew she was off work tonight. She wanted me to stay home for a movie night, but I was too eager to see Perry. I would just call her back soon. A sudden wave of sadness washed over me, and a lone tear fell from my eye. I felt my face crumple up and my lip tremble, all ready for a good sob before I caught myself and bit down hard on my bottom lip.

"Now is not the time to fall apart, Sinclair. She was just busy, that's all. Give it a minute."

Giving myself a little shake, I pushed myself up and onto my feet.

"So, dark night, big house, alone, with a massive storm. What do you do first?"

Right. Checklist time. *What should I be doing?*

Well, am I safe here? Right –Need to finish inspecting the house.

Next? Is there any water or heat source? Any bathroom usable? Yep-that makes sense. *Water, heat, check for a bathroom.*

Mental checklist done, I had a plan of action, at least. I thought I was alone, but there could be squatters or something, maybe tweakers passed out somewhere. Best to make sure. Couldn't hurt to see if there was any running water or find a blanket or two.

I knew nothing about fireplaces, so starting a fire was out. I didn't want to fill the place with smoke. I shrugged, glancing sadly at the stone hearth. I'm sure it was beautiful when lit. I picked up my makeshift candlestick and my phone and headed to the stairs.

TO MY RELIEF, THE stairs were solid beneath my feet; the marble littered with dried leaves and flower petals. The banister was cold under my grip, dusty and filmed with cobwebs, but still sturdy. My sneakers crunched over the leaves as I padded softly upstairs. Fear wasn't gripping me, but anxiety was. I had announced my presence when I entered. No one answered. Not a sound came from within, but in my mind as I advanced up the marble, all manner of rodents and squatters were hiding around every corner.

I smirked slightly as the images ran unbidden through my brain. One too many horror movies growing up will do that to a person. I swept the thin beam of my flashlight across the top landing as I reached it. The corridor stretched out along both sides of the house, shadowed doorways waiting to swallow me whole as I hesitated. I chose the left side and began my investigation.

I played the light over the hallway, sweeping it along the walls and ceiling, and back down. Cobwebs hung like a silk thread from the corners of high beams and light fixtures. Leaves danced along my path, caught in the motion of my steps, skittering across the floor as I walked. The first doorway was a large bathroom.

I stepped across the threshold, holding the candle

out as I went, the flashlight pointed at my feet. More marble floor in here, or maybe tile of some sort, lined the floor. It gleamed in the low light, despite the dirt and debris of past decades. A massive clawfoot tub stood across from me, with double sinks on the left wall, topped with a gilt-edge mirror. I gasped, then quickly recovered as I realized that it was only a mirror with my own image looking back at me. I chuckled and set the candle down on the sink edge. My auburn hair clung to my face from rain and sweat, the curls just starting to become wild and frizzy.

My brown eyes studied my reflection, shining in the candlelight. My bottom lip was red from chewing on it and I licked it with the tip of my tongue, soothing the wound even as my teeth bit into it once more. My clothes were slightly damp but clean. The plain black t-shirt and jean shorts seemed plain and frumpy now, hardly suitable for a hot beach date. I sighed and pushed my hair back from my face, using an elastic from my pocket to tie it back in a messy ponytail. I glanced down at the sink, reminding myself why I was here, and tested the water faucets, then the commode.

The toilet flushed, startling me as I pulled the chain on the wall, not expecting anything, but it flushed all the same. As it did, water gurgled to life in the twin basins beneath the mirror. I looked and grimaced at the murky liquid as it trickled, then increased to a stream, then cleared.

Well, that's something, I thought to myself. At least

I can pee. I waited a few minutes, testing to see if the water would get warm, but knowing that would be pushing my luck. There was no way a water heater was still functioning in this mammoth tomb of an era long-gone.

I moved from that space, grateful to know that there was water. I wouldn't have to squat over a rancid bowl filled with sludge nor find a corner to piss in like a hobo. The next door hid a linen closet with shelves still full of moth-eaten towels, blankets, and bedsheets. I coughed as a wave of dust drifted out, then took a blanket from the shelf, inspecting it at arm's length, shaking it out the best I could, which only added to the flurry of debris in the air and my coughing fit. Holes covered it, so I let it drop to the next shelf and tried another one. Several tries later, I found a quilt that had held up over time quite well. It would do for the night. I draped it over my shoulder and closed the door, moving on down the hallway.

The next two doors held bedroom suites, large rooms with four-poster beds, enormous closets, and a bathroom in-between. The décor seemed suitable for a child; maybe young girls had resided in these two rooms. Faded wallpaper still had pale images of roses with pink ribbons swirled within and along the border. Dainty picture frames lined the dresser. A silver brush and hand-mirror lay on the vanity, the polish blurred and faded with age. The closets still held rows of dresses and coats.

I moved along, no longer worried about intruders,

too impressed with the décor that just begged to be appreciated. The furniture was well made, most likely hand carved. Each piece was as ornate as the luxurious dining room ensemble downstairs. I walked through the bathroom, finding another clawfoot tub with double sinks and the same commode with the pull chain. I stepped through to the next bedroom, finding a replica of the one I had just been in, except daisy wallpaper clung to these walls. Faded yellow paint adorned the vanity, and many of the dresses were yellow or carried shades of yellow in them.

Being the girl that I am, I automatically decided the rose room belonged to a teen, while the Daisy room belonged to a younger girl, maybe nine or ten years old. Rose and Daisy, I repeated to myself, naming them as I left the room. I smiled. Maybe that was their names, it could be, why not? I shrugged, smiling. I had a quirk for naming things, all things. I stepped into the hallway and crossed over to the next room, just at the far end.

This room was smaller, set up to serve as both a playroom and classroom. Rows of books lined one wall, two desks sat in the middle, and several shelves of toys lined the back wall. One window above the toy shelf allowed a single beam of moonlight into the room, casting pale shadows on everything. I went to the books, inspecting them, tilting my head in that curious pose that only true readers are accustomed to, and read the spines. Twain, Dickens, Poe, Frost, Dickinson, Browning, and Longfellow lined the shelves.

Jane Eyre, Dorian Gray, Alice's Adventures in Wonderland, The Jungle Book, and Dracula were all here, along with many others. I gingerly lifted several volumes, blew the dust away, and peered at the first few pages. These were first editions, and most seemed to be in great shape. The books here were probably worth a small fortune. I replaced them carefully and moved along, picking my candle up from the desk once again. No rodents. No squatters. Nothing to fear, at least not within these rooms. I padded quietly down the hallway once more to the other side, ready to finish my tour and retire to the main library downstairs to wait out the storm.

THE REMAINING ROOMS ON the opposite end held a small study, two rather plain guest rooms decorated with violet wallpaper. Each bedroom still held furniture, a dressing table, a desk, and a hand-carved four-poster bed. Closets lined the back wall of each, and a bathroom connected the rooms, just like the rose and daisy rooms. The study held rows of bookshelves, full of ancient tomes of literature and knowledge. The desk was a smaller version of the one that sat in the library downstairs.

The master suite was last; a beautiful series of connecting rooms full of mahogany furniture, deep crimson and gold paper adorned the walls, and heavy oriental carpets covered the floors. The bathroom was connected to the bedroom by an elaborate dressing room, closest on each side, with an ornate vanity table and bench in the middle. I whistled softly, looking around the room. It was impressive, even draped in cobwebs and filmed by layers of dirt. I felt an odd sense of trespassing just being in here, more so than being in the house in general.

This was the owners' room, their bedroom. The masters of the domain and somehow forbidden to everyone else. I didn't know why I knew that, but I knew it all the same. This was their sanctuary. I left the room quietly, properly cowed by the sheer display of wealth and luxury that coated the room, matching the rest of the house, but much more elaborate than any other of the bedrooms.

I headed back to the staircase, candle and blanket in hand. As I descended, I felt an odd sensation creep over me, as if someone was watching, but when I glanced back, nothing was around. The sense of heaviness lifted as I descended the steps, and I breathed easier when I reached the first floor. The air was lighter here, probably from the massive gusts of wind I had let in upon my entry. I went to the library and set the blanket on the chaise I had claimed for the evening, then checked my phone. Still no messages from my mom. I sighed and sent another quick message to her, then shut off the device to save what little power I had left.

My stomach rumbled loudly as I stood in the room, trying to decide what to do next. I rubbed my stomach, then wandered from the room toward the kitchen in the back of the house. It didn't have much but there was water, and I spotted some tea bags earlier. At least it would be something. I held the candle at chest level to help light the hallway. Eerie shadows played across the walls, skeletal tree branches scratched at the windows outside and cast long fingers across the dim corridor. Lightning lit the backyard, and I froze for a second as a figure was made visible in the shadows. Tall, slender, and feminine. Then it was gone.

I gasped and held the candle higher, waiting to see it again, waiting for lightning to illuminate the yard once more, but neither happened. Thunder boomed, and I jumped, yelping loudly from the sudden shock. Every muscle in my body tensed and I inched forward on silent feet, hoping that it was just bushes and trees in the yard, casting shadowy shapes and figures in the moonlight. I had seen no sign of any human inhabitants or rodents during my investigation of the upper floor. It had to be a trick of the light.

I scolded myself for being silly and reached the kitchen without further incident. It had been a long day, and my nerves were already shot. It was no wonder that I had been spooked so easily. I set the candle down on the counter and opened the cupboard that I had rummaged through earlier. Spying the tea and sugar, I snagged them and set them on the counter. I looked again, stretching on tip-toe to see the upper shelf. Several cans of soup were there, so I grabbed a chicken noodle, hoping it wasn't rancid, and set that down too.

Seeing as how there was a giant sink, running water, and I had matches, maybe I could warm it up somehow. Hopefully, the soup was still good. I knew canned goods lasted quite a while. My stomach rumbled again. I sighed and patted it, then started opening drawers, looking for a small pot I could use.

Lightning lit the yard once more and I spun around, staring through the windows to the yard, trying to see the same shape I saw before, but nothing was there that could explain it. The trees were enormous oaks, mostly lining the back and sides of the lawn. Nothing stood in the middle where the figure had been, not even a flower bush. I shuddered as that heavy feeling returned. Ice gripped my spine and chills caused goosebumps to break out on my arms. I rubbed them briskly and returned to my search.

Hopefully warm soup and tea would settle my nerves, and morning would come quickly. I suddenly wanted to be out of this house, but the storm raged outside, and the temperature had dropped drastically. Leaving now was not an option.

CHAPTER THREE

I RUMMAGED THROUGH THE pots and pans until I found a cast-iron pot and a cooling rack for cakes. I snagged a small saucepan too and carried my items to the sink. I set the pot down on the stove, then looked around for a bit of trash I might be able to use to start a fire in the pot. Several cabinets later, I had a couple of brittle napkins, a box of toothpicks and two half broken wooden spoons. I shrugged. Good enough, I thought. Wood burns, right?

I added the items to the pot, started the fire using the napkins and waited for my wooden pieces to catch fire. Once they did, I set the rack over the top, filled the saucepan with water and placed it on the rack. I pulled the tab open on the soup and set that on the rack as well, next to the saucepan. If my fire lasted long enough, I'd have hot tea and soup for dinner. I smirked a little as I roamed the kitchen, proud of my creative cooking attempt.

Cobwebs swayed from the high corners. Most of the kitchen appliances all seemed to be here. Most of everything still seemed to be here. I couldn't make sense of why no one had come to pack the house after the last owner died. I assumed they died. If they had just moved, why not pack their belongings? Maybe no family left to care, I mused as I leafed through vintage recipe books and idly pulled open the many drawers lining the wall of cabinets.

The drawers held all the normal items, old coupon booklets, matches, and a few more candles. Serving utensils filled another drawer, real silver ones judging by the state of them. A good polish would clean those up nicely. The silver in the drawers had to be worth a small fortune on their own. I shook my head again and turned back to the stove. Why so much wealth and no one to claim it? No one at all to leave it too? That was a sad way to end a life if that were to be true. I sincerely hoped it wasn't.

Slight wisps of flames were licking the edge of the pot, but not enough to alarm me. Smoke was starting to drift through the room, though, so I headed to the back door. The porch was enclosed with screens so I could safely let the smoke out without letting any-thing in. The storm still raged just beyond the porch. I cautiously unlocked the door, stuck my head out to make sure no rodents were about to ambush me, and stepped onto the porch to look around. The screens all seemed intact.

Lightning struck again in the middle of the yard and there stood another blobby shadow. I gasped and backed away, immediately unsettled by the shape. There, and gone, in the sudden flash of blue light. I stepped back into the kitchen, leaving the door open only the smallest crack to let the smoke out. I waited, counting seconds as the thunder rolled again. Another flash, but nothing was there. I squinted harder into the gloomy yard and waited once more. Maybe it was just a strange shadow, I thought, trying to justify what I had seen not once, but three times now.

The hell with this, I thought. I shut the door and locked it. Hot or not, the water and soup would have to do. I filled another pot with water from the sink and dumped it over the small fire. Steam hissed and rose, and the flames went out. I was pleased to see that the water for my tea was indeed starting to bubble, which meant it was at least somewhat hot, as would be the soup. My stomach growled, and I turned to rummage around for a towel to move the soup can and a spoon.

I found what I needed, poured the soup into a mug, water in another one and added the tea and sugar. Satisfied with my meager meal and checking that the flames were out, I left the kitchen, returning to the library to eat and count the minutes until morning. Darkness and the rumble of thunder followed me along with a sense of loneliness that made me want my mom more than ever before.

SETTLING IN ON THE dusty chaise in the library, I curled my feet beneath me and slowly ate the lukewarm soup. My first bite was tentative, tasting for any sign of rancidness, but it smelled and tasted fine. I said a silent prayer that my senses were not deceiving me and continued to eat while gazing around the room. Streaks of lightning lit up the room every few minutes, filtering in through the cracks in the boards outside.

Eerie shadows played across the walls and rows of bookshelves and the wind blew against the house, making an unsettling wailing noise. I tried to block out the noise and shadows and comforted myself with my soup and the mug of tea.

"It could be worse." I said out loud, "you could be outside, stuck in that downpour, still trudging down a dark road."

My voice sounded small and lonely in the vast room, bouncing off the high ceiling. I took a sip of the tea, not wanting it to cool off too quickly. My stomach was comfortably warm and full, and the chill was slowly leaving my bones.

"You are alone. You have food. You have water. You are dry." More affirmations said out loud, nodding as I processed each one. It could be much worse. Sure, it was a creepy house with a disturbing shadow in the back beneath the trees, flickering in and out of existence with every flash of lightning, but I was *inside.* That had to count for something, right?

I nodded again, mildly angry that I was allowing my imagination to run wild. I was a strong, capable adult and surely, I could survive one night in an old house. I was being silly, that's all, childish and silly. I scolded myself, pulled my cell phone back out and checked it. I had about nine percent battery life left, so I shot my mom a quick text. Explained my situation briefly, assured her that I was okay and said I would leave early in the morning to find a way to call her.

I allowed myself two minutes to wait for a reply, but when none came, I powered the phone back down. Hopefully, she would see my message and wouldn't worry. I didn't know exactly where I was, somewhere off route 68. I told her where we had come from before Perry stranded me and I tried to describe the house that I was in and the old diner I had passed several miles back. If she did try to call for help, at least she had some description to give them.

Another clap of thunder shook the house, and I jumped as the lightning struck just a second later. Across the room, in the darkest corner, a shadow loomed, tall and wraithlike. My heart raced as I stared at it, mouth dry, eyes locked on, afraid to move. I stood there, frozen in fear, counting the seconds for the thunder, for the lightning, for anything to happen to show me that it was gone, that it wasn't real.

The candles flickered once, twice, then grew steady

once more. Another booming roll of thunder crashed overhead, and lightning stretched long, bright blue fingers into the room. The shadow was gone. I blinked and waited, not allowing myself to breathe. A third wave of storm-borne chaos struck thunder, rattling the old glass in its pane. The sudden flash showed an empty corner, nothing but heavy drapes pooled on the floor and a tall lamp between the two shelves there.

I relaxed and breathed, gasping slightly as my lungs gulped in air. I scolded myself again as I moved to lift one candle from the end table.

"Damnit Sinclair, get a grip." I muttered.

I padded over to the corner on shaky legs, needing to see for myself that draperies and lamp legs were all I had to fear. Holding the candle high, I moved toward it, navigating chairs, shelves, and tables as I went. Cobwebs drifted from chandeliers, wisping across my neck and face. I swatted them away, not needing any more chills tonight.

I turned slowly in a circle, lifting the curtains, peering behind them, looking for anything that may have made the shadow that I saw, but nothing made sense. The hairs on the back of my neck stood up as a chill washed over me, cold like ice, raising goosebumps down both arms. A shudder ran down my spine as I backed away. Whatever this was, I didn't like it.

Turning as calmly as I could, I went back to my side of the room, sitting on the edge of the chaise. I turned slightly so I could keep that corner in my line of sight as I tried to decide what to do.

"Get it together, damnit. It's an old drafty house in the middle of a rainstorm. That's all. There are no ghosts. No demons. No spirits. Just you, the rain, and a couple of drafty windows." I chided myself, trying to make the chill in my spine go away. My hands shook, and I squeezed them together between my legs.

Closing my eyes, I focused on counting to one hundred, breathing slowly and deeply as I did so. I refused to give in to my fear. I was stressed out from my day. It was a creepy house and bad weather, nothing more. I opened my eyes and screamed.

CHAPTER FOUR

THE SHADOW WAS BACK, clearly outlined in front of the windows. The heavy fabric of the draperies pooled on either side of it, while the figure hovered in the middle. Lightning struck right outside, once, twice, illuminating the entire room. There it stood, tall, feminine, shrouded in skirts and veils of darkness. I gasped. I rose swiftly to my feet and darted from the room. Up the stairs I ran, taking them two at a time, refusing to look back. Whatever it was, could have the library.

I darted to the right at the top, down the hall to the master bedroom, and slammed the door closed. I leaned against it, shaking and panting. My lungs were on fire. My throat hurt from the shriek I had uttered only seconds before. I did not think myself capable of such a scream until that very moment. As my heart found its way back into my chest where it belonged, I blinked, looking around me, slowly realizing that I had trapped myself in the pitch black room. The candles were downstairs.

I straightened, stepping away from the door, patting my pockets, hoping I had my cell and hadn't left it on the chaise in my flight. With a sigh of relief, my fingers found the hard shape in my back pocket. I pulled it free, powered it on, and pressed the flashlight button, sweeping the thin beam around the room. It looked just as it had before. Imposing, but empty. No wraiths backlit by the raging storm.

I stepped over to the wall of windows across the room and swept the velvet draperies to the side, hoping for a sliver of moonlight to ease the suffocating blackness of the room. The storm was angry and violent outside. The trees in the yard were almost bowed to the ground by the winds. Rain pelted the house and the windows, sounding like hail and sleet rather than the driving rain that it was. A long finger of pale light filtered through the trees and fell across the room in a single swath, neatly cutting the suite in half.

The light glinted on the closet door, on the brass knobs that served to open it. Another clap of thunder shook the walls, and I scooted away from the windows. Not knowing what to do next or what to think about my predicament, I wandered across the room and sat on the floor, directly in the moonlight, back against the closet door.

I faced the magnificent four-poster bed and wished

it still held a mattress. Maybe if I could just sleep, I would be free of this nightmare sooner. I had to be seeing things; I told myself. Ghosts didn't exist. There was no woman haunting these halls, no midnight wraith stalking me from room to room. It was stress, and shock and fear, and the fury of the storm outside. A perfect combination to trigger an overactive imagination. With my knees pulled up to my chest, I folded my arm around them and rested my head on them. Not wanting to close my eyes, I found myself gazing beneath the bed slats.

My private moonbeam fell across several of the slats before it soaked me in its ray and the closet door behind me. Something glinted between the rails on the far side, tucked between the slats and frame. A dangle of ribbon hung just below the board, sticking out of something above it. Curious, I scooted closer and stared a bit harder. I certainly didn't want to disturb a rat nest or a mouse.

I waited for another streak of lightning and watched as it lit the room. There seemed to be a book wedged into that tight space, a slender one with a bit of ribbon inside. I rose to my feet and made my way around the bed to the far side. Once there, I used my flashlight again to see better as I dug my hand into the space between the wood. My fingers grazed a thin, leather–bound book. I tugged at it and wrenched it free.

The word "Diary" was stamped across it in a fancy lettering. It had a ragged bit of twine wrapped around it twice, tucked in to hold it closed, and a faded red ribbon poking from the top. Dust covered it and the leather was cracked, dry and brittle with age. I carefully opened it to see sloping feminine handwriting covering the pages. Curiosity had me in its clutches now. Maybe I would discover more about who lived here while I waited for morning. I retreated to my pool of moonlight and began reading.

Oak Helm Manor- October 10, 1920

IT'S BEEN COLD TODAY, colder than last fall. Jonathan says it's normal for this time of year here near the coast, but I don't remember last October being quite so cold so soon. Of course, I was busy with Lilah most of that time. Poor sweet Lilah, so sick but how cheerful she was, all the way until the last moment. My poor sweet girl. I ache for her so, even now. Months have passed, and I can still smell her sweet smell. The scent of her hair, her skin damp with fever, the wildflowers that always sat on her vanity, keeping the room bright. Days like today, I fear my heart may break and never recover.

The dreams were awful last night. So horrid, I woke screaming in my bed. Jonathan stood over me, shaking me. The worry on his face only made me feel worse. I had disturbed his rest once more. He worked so hard these days, working with his father, watching over the manor, watching over me. Always watching someone, somewhere, but he hadn't been watching Lilah, had he? The one time that he should have been watching, needed to be watching, he had looked away.

By the time they realized she was missing, it was almost too late. Her lips were blue. Her dress and shoes soaked through. Her slender frame shook in my arms for hours that night. The water in the well had been cold, frigid, so deep in the ground. It had taken the men hours to retrieve her from the dark pit in the ground. Jonathan was to have that well filled in, but he had forgotten, time and time again. Oh, my dear sweet Lilah, I'd give anything to hear you laugh again. To see your bright smile. My heart hurts. It bleeds naught but tears for you every day, my sweet darling girl.

I know Jonathan blames himself. I know I should not, but there's a part of me that cannot help it. A small anger bitter part of me that looks at him differently now over dinner and tea. A vengeful part of me that wishes it was he that had fallen instead of our daughter. How horrible I sound. How cruel must I be?

She was his child, too. He must be grieving, too. Certainly, he is. I have been told that there is nothing quite like the grief of a mother when she loses her child. The very being she gave life to, gave her body *to, housed and sheltered and nurtured within herself for months. And then to watch that very same life, that sacrifice of time and pain and love and care to slowly fade from eyes that look just like yours?*

Eyes that stare into yours and beg silently for relief, beg for a respite from the pain and the fevers and the shaking within her very bones that caused tears to leak from her eyes every hour of every day. What was I to do? What could I do? Oh god, what was I to do?

THE PASSAGE ENDED THERE, several smears led to blank lines and then the next page. I sat quietly for a moment, not realizing that the house had gone silent. The storm had passed on while I read the brittle journal. Such a sad passage to start with. Idly, I wondered if the child was the one; I had nicknamed Rose, or maybe Daisy? My wandering through the house earlier had led me to believe that the girls were sisters and, based solely on the décor of their bedroom walls, I had named them Daisy and Rose.

Daisy, in my mind, was the younger of the two, and if I was understanding the journal, then one of the children had fallen in a well. This sounds fitting for a younger child, not a teen. Based on the clothing I had found in their rooms, Rose was an older girl, which meant Daisy would be the child that had passed away. My heart hurt for the woman, just imagining the loss. I gently turned the page, curious to see if the woman continued on in such a manner.

Clearly, guilt and despair still weighed heavily on the woman, anger for her husband as well. Such things were natural reactions. This was understood now, in our time, but was it understood in theirs? My brain repeated those last lines on a loop. "*What had she done? And to whom?*" I mused softly to myself as I leaned against the closet door again and turned to the next page.

Oak Helm Manor– October 14, 1920

I AWOKE FROM THE dreams again, my poor Lilah's face screaming at me from beneath a pool of rippling waters. Water that I could not reach, a surface that I could not breach. I tried again and again to reach her. I plunged my arms into the well, over and over, up to my elbows I did, but they came out dry every time. Not a drop of water on them, not a new ripple on the surface where my Lilah screamed for mercy just beneath. Naught for me to do but watch her drown with useless lungs, and useless hands, and a useless empty heart.

God, take it from my chest. I do not want this pain any longer. Take it from me while it still beats. Take it and let me die, let me cease, mercy I beg of you, the pain is too great. I woke, sobbing and sobbing and sobbing. Jonathan looks at me with disdain and despair in his eyes. He does not know how to feel. This pain is alien to him. Men are not taught to grieve, to feel as we feel. They are not taught how to cling to that ache, so you remember that you were once alive. That you were once whole and full and vibrant and complete. They do not know that after such a loss, a loss such as this, the pain is all you know. You cannot move on from it. You do not wish it gone. You do not wish to be free of it. Indeed, it is your only reminder that you exist. That you still live and breathe, that your bones still feel life, that your lungs still pull oxygen from the air; that your heart still beats within your chest, even though you are too numb to feel it.

The pain, the pain, is all there is, all you have left. The pain is a need now, our most sacred craving, pain, pain, pain, pain, and nothing more. The pain is our heartbeat. The pain reminds us to breathe. I do so now, gasping and sobbing and screaming for her, for my Lilah, my sweet lost Lilah. Jonathan leaves the room as I cling to my madness, thrashing about the sheets in my anguish. Nary a kind word or soft hand to calm me as he passes. Naught but quiet refusal to acknowledge that I exist. I quiet, and I begin to question, do I exist? Did he even see me? Did he hear me at all? Or have I passed on too?

Passed on from this place, seeking solace, seeking Lilah, wandering through the purgatory of these endless halls crying out for my daughter to answer me, to laugh just once more. But there is nothing but silence here. Even Mae lingers in the shadows, uneasy around me. Her pale face sticks to her chambers, her classroom, her books. The swish of her skirts is all I hear as she passes me, head down, footsteps dainty as Nanny ushers her along.

Mae must be sorrowful too, her lovely sister gone from us far too soon, her mother, too distraught to notice her illness, her weakness, the way she has grown pale, the skin pulled taut over bones and sunken over cheeks. The way her dresses hang from her frame, the dark pockets that ring her eyes beneath the powder that Nanny has swept across cheek and collarbone to try to disguise. My own child, wasting away before my own eyes. My unseeing, unblinking, unrealizing eyes.

Despair was eating Mae alive, swallowing her whole, bit by bit. Jonathan is a ghost. He does not linger here, not in these vacant halls where his wife and daughter dwell, both drowning in sorrow, locked in private hells. Nanny ushers her along, silent glares and haughty judgment as I glide down the gloomy corridors. I do not speak, nor do I nod. The only sign of my passing is the soft patter of blood on the floor like teardrops as I grip the razor blade hidden in my palm. The pain, my new heartbeat, reminding me I'm alive. I grip it. I gasp. I breathe. I cry. My heart beats once more.

I CLOSED THE BOOK when I noticed the tears splattering on the page. My own tears. My shoulders heave as the dam breaks and I allow the grief to flow through. Her grief, and my own. Her suffering, her daughters, her heartbreak and mine. I collapse to the floor, clinging to the skirts of her dresses that hang low in the closet, and I weep for her losses and my own. A raw pain fills my soul, and it's like nothing that I have ever felt before. I know the pain that she speaks of, how to feel what she is feeling. We do carry it within us, in a way that many others do not. A tidal wave of emotions wash over me, anguish and despair, hurt and loss and so much sorrow and regret.

As I cried, I understood that I carried the weight of a generation within me, but how and why? Was I meant to be here somehow? Was I connected to this lady of sorrow? Was it she that roamed this place, seeking her daughters? I felt the fear lift from me then and only felt sorrow and compassion for this matriarch of the manor. What a sad life she must have led. Long minutes later, I rose to my feet and, carrying the diary with me, I descended to the library, more confident than before in knowing what roamed these halls and why.

I ENTERED THE LIBRARY a little more reverently than I had left it, fleeing in fear from what I now thought to be the presence of the grieving lady of the house. The black gown and veil that shadowed her countenance were of the right style and design to match the years noted in the diary, the very same as the moth-eaten dresses that still filled the closets upstairs. Setting the diary down on the mahogany table next to the chaise I had claimed, I lit a fresh candle from the ones I had gathered and set it beside the first.

Lighting two more, I carried these to the dark corners of the room, hoping to chase away some of the shadows. Rain pelted the house outside, wind screamed through the treetops, creating a haunting banshee wail in the night. A chill ran up my spine at the muffled sound, and I was grateful to be inside for the night, safe from the storm. Much of my fear had left me but, in its place, a heavy feeing of apprehension and curiosity had settled in my bones.

What more might the lady do while I took shelter here? What other secrets might her diary reveal? A neglectful husband, but perhaps he was only misunderstood? Lost in his own grief and sense of failed duty as a father and husband? And what of Mae, the older girl? How deep her sorrow must be? Not able to help her parents, not able to help herself, spending her days clinging to the care of a nanny and the cold corners of the manor. What other horrors had she witnessed?

I sighed and stood up, restless and growing thirsty. I took a candle and retraced my steps to the kitchen. Repeating my process from earlier in the evening, I lit a small fire in the heavy pot once more and set the pan of water on top to heat. Tea would soothe both my throat and the cold seeping into my flesh. I rummaged through the cabinet once more for another tea bag and the sugar and set those aside, then turned to the back door.

The thunder rolled as I opened the door again and stepped onto the enclosed porch, peering out across the black lawn beyond. The trees reached for the house, bony branches bending, swaying, and scratching at the gables, the chimneys, the windows, and walls. Scraping and raking across board, brick, and stone, adding to the cacophony of the storm. Young saplings along the pathways bent low, bowing in an informal curtsy as I gazed at the yard. Bolts of lightning flashed overhead, illuminating the grounds in bursts of light and color for seconds at a time.

Stone statues ringed a fountain in the middle of the grass. Lined pathways led to it and branched off to either side and behind it. Remnants of what looked like a garden sat to the far left, while wildly overgrown bushes lined the fence on the right, rose bushes, if I guessed correctly. My imagination filled the estate lawn with a riot of color, flowers blooming, vegetables of all kinds creeping up the garden poles and along the rows, green ivy slithering and writhing up the edges of the manor and the trees.

Visitors in fine dress walking the paths, tea being served near the marble foundation filled with clear water, maybe a party or a gathering for an occasion. The yard lit up at that moment and I could almost see my vision clearly in the split second of light. I smiled, amused at my wild imaginings, then turned to check the water for my tea when she appeared once more.

Tall and unmoving, she stood directly in front of the fountain path. Veiled and gowned, no features that I could see, just her outline and a movement. A single lift of her arm, a delicate hand pointed to the left, where the rose bushes strangled the fence line. That was all. I blinked, and she was gone. I stared hard into the night, refusing to move my eyes from the spot where she had been. I waited for her to appear again, but she did not. There was naught but a crash of thunder to jolt me from my paralysis and another streak of blue electricity that shattered the sky.

I stepped away from the porch, leaving the door ajar slightly to allow the smoke to escape. I tended to the small fire and made my tea, leaving the pot of water to sit atop the other, hopefully to keep warm for a while longer. My mind raced and my hands shook as I stirred the tea. She had pointed at something. I knew it. This was no trick of the light. No shadows from the storm. She was there, and she was talking to me.

Should I go outside? Brave this weather to see what her message was meant to be? Maybe read another entry in her journal first? I didn't know what to do next, read or follow her plea? Sitting still and drinking my tea and waiting for morning seemed to be the rational choice, but what about tonight had been rational at all?

CHAPTER FIVE

Sipping the hot tea from the safety of the porch, I stood staring across the yard. The storm raged on, branches bent low, bowing as I gazed at them. Rain pelted the house. Lightning streaked through the sky every few seconds and illuminated the earth beneath as I waited for the wraith to appear again. The sudden thudding of an object crashing to the floor beyond the kitchen caught my attention, and I turned back toward the interior of the house, startled. A second later, a deafening clap of thunder made my decision for me, and I scurried from the kitchen down the hallway to the only room I found comfort in.

I hissed as the tea splashed my fingers, shaking the few drops away as I entered the room. I set the cup carefully down on the table near the candles I had left burning and looked around the room. My gaze found the source of the noise rather quickly as my feet kicked the object and sent it skittering across the floor. The journal was there, mere feet away from where I stood. I had left it on the tableside when I went to the kitchen, but here it was, face up, on the floor.

No longer believing in coincidences at this particular moment, I picked it up gingerly, keeping my finger on the open page so it wouldn't flutter closed as I sat down on the chaise once more. I scooted closer to the candlelight and studied the page. It wasn't the page that I had stopped my reading on, but a few pages after it; a week beyond the last entry I had read.

Oak Helm Manor–October 25, 1920

MAE IS GONE. MY child, my only remaining child, is gone from this earth. Wasted away to naught but bone and sunken, sad eyes. I cannot cry. There are no tears left. How could there be? Lilah is gone. Jonathan might as well be a phantom in this house. I barely exist at all. Only Nanny remains mortal flesh, healthy and fat, skin glowing like roses, a child deep within her womb. Her time approaches and I cannot bear the sight of her. Her happiness chasing the darkest shadows away, save for when she sees me in the corridors. Then, the smile fades, turns to polite distrust and a modicum of fear. I have been harsh with her since of late.

Blaming her for my own fate, for Lilah's, now for Mae's. Was it not Nanny charged with her care? With her meals? With her learning? Is it not my fault that Nanny failed us all? Even now, she fails me. Singing cheerily in the kitchen as she prepares the meal. This is a house of mourning. How dare she disrespect the grief that we are feeling? Mourners are coming tomorrow to sit in wake for Mae but there is no chance of that. The child will not wake. She will not breathe, nor blink, nor twitch. I've been staring at her body for hours as the night passed by. Not a strand of hair on her head has moved. Not a soft moan of pain, or a feverish groan. My child, my daughter, is dead. And it's Nanny's fault.

I stare at Jonathan when he enters the room, silent and pale, regretful and prideful at once. His shame reflected in the firelight, in his eyes, in the very air of the room. Here surrounded by books, by truth from ages far behind us, he has yet to confront his own. His children, dead. His wife, neglected. The housekeeper, fat with his child. The very shame of it will bury us all. My eyes narrow as I meet his stormy gray ones over the rim of my wineglass. He thinks I do not know. I will die before I speak of such.

I'd rather die. I'd rather he die. I know how he should die. Out in that well, broken and drowning in mud, like our Lilah. Alone and suffering for hours as her life bled into the earth. That's how he should die. But also then, should not I?

My heart is broken. I fear my mind may be too. Is this normal thought to have against one's husband? Against one's servant and maid? Is this grief? No one ever told me that life would be like this. Why hadn't Mother told me? Why hadn't Father told me of the hurt and the pain and fear and the lies? Why do we not prepare our children for this life? All pretty rainbows and sugar-coated lies.

I SAT BACK ON the chaise, chilled to the bone. The anguish was almost too much to bear. I could feel her pain emanating from the pages of the journal. The wind shrieked outside and to me; it sounded far too much like a wail of loss and sorrow. I sniffed and wiped my eyes, only then realizing that I had been crying. Her words had not been lost on me, even drowning in the despair of her words. I knew where I needed to look. I only needed to work up the nerve. The well that sat beyond the fountain in the yard, near the rosebushes that climbed the rear fence. The well that taken their Lilah. The well that Jonathan had neglected to cover.

I picked the journal up once more, wanting to read

further before I made my decision. Deep down, I knew I was only delaying the inevitable. I knew I would find myself outside facing the storm. My heart begged to question if the storm out there would be safer than the one brewing within the manor. I could feel her presence even now. Heavy and oppressive sadness filled the air, mixed with a deep longing. I felt it weighing on me. I knew that I could not bear that kind of despair for long, knowing the lady of the manor had endured it for decades without end was heartbreaking.

I drew the candle closer to the table's edge and curled my legs up on the couch and began to read again.

Oak Helm Manor–October 28, 1920

I fear I have damned myself to Hell. To whatever infernal torture waits for me upon my death. I have committed the unthinkable. The worst sin of all. My hands were strange, uncontrollable beasts consumed by a savage rage. Even as my mind screamed No in terror and despair, my heart, my body, did what they desired without qualm, without thought, without guilt, until now. Guilt overwhelms me. Frantic thoughts spiral through my mind. I've not slept in days for fear of my discovery, rather, fear of my crime being discovered.

First my darling girls, and now this awful, dreadful thing. Nanny has fled. I watched her go from beneath the Garrett windows. I stood tall, framed by the glass as the sky turned the color of fresh bruises and decay, yellow and purple in the west. She never turned back. Heavy with their child, a satchel in hand, she wobbled on shaky legs to the car that waited for her. Then and only then did she glance up, up to the window where I stood. I stiffened. My eyes narrowed. My heart filled with frozen daggers that I could not shoot. My mouth twisted with anger, vile words that a lady should not utter spewed from my wretched tongue. Only the glass pane kept my words at bay, spat like venom from the deadliest of snakes. "Be gone, you wretch! Be gone, you vile seductress!!"

I shrieked with all the force my broken body had left within. Tears spilled from my eyes. Hate twisted my visage. My hair unfurled from its prim style, twisted upon my neck. I raged. I screamed. I hurled insults and epithets until my voice gave out and blood poured from my throat. I woke, hours later, collapsed on the floor. Shattered glass surrounded me. My palms were covered in crimson. Shards stuck my dress, my hands, my face. Blood lingered in my mouth, coppery and clotted. I looked at myself as I rose, the antique mirror in the cobwebbed corner reflecting my shame. This evil, wretched thing I had become, this shadow of what remained. I had been a lady of dignity and grace. A proper hostess, a good daughter and dutiful wife. Well-rounded, educated, and tamed, now I was this wild and feral thing. I turned from the mirror with a tortured cry and fled to my chambers. Alone in this manor, abandoned by all that I held dear. I fled to the darkened rooms of my boudoir and there I stayed.

My HANDS SHOOK AS I set the diary down beside me. Her pain was so great, so overwhelming, that my heart ached with it. Grief and anguish poured from her words like an ocean of tears. Ink stained saltwater ran across brittle pages of parchment in an attempt to free herself of the despair she found herself trapped in. I shuddered as a chill danced up my spine, winding across my torso like vines of ivy. The candles flickered, and I glanced sharply to my left to watch, breath catching in my throat as I waited to see if the light would hold. Frosty plumes of frigid air drifted from my lips and nostrils as the realization struck me that it was not the chill of the story being told in the journal that drenched my bones in ice, but rather the plummeting temperature of the room itself. The flames flickered twice more, and a low moan emitted from my throat. I felt my eyes widen.

My stomach twisted around the leaden ball of dread that filled it. Fear, horror, and a keen sense of empathy twisted my emotions into knots as I stared at the morose visage of the lady of the manor. She glided toward me from the far corner, all shade and shadows, rather than flesh and bone. Her eyes were empty sockets. Her cheeks, sunken, framed by a sharp jawline, a stern chin and high furrowed brow. Graying strands of hair hung limply from the once elegant bun atop her head. The dress of black chiffon and lace rustled as she stopped a few feet from me. Her left arm rose, slowly, ever so slowly. Those horrible eyes stared into my soul as that arm stopped and her finger lifted to the point.

Seconds past. Time seemed to stop. I hung there suspended in limbo, fright seized my every limb, paralyzed the breath in my chest. A single tear drifted from my eye as her stare kept me rooted in place. Then she screamed, suddenly moving right toward me, mouth open and unhinged, dropping almost to her collarbone, impossibly wide. Inches from my face, she screamed. The fetid breath washed across my face, decay and rot and dank putrescence decades in the making seared my nostrils, choking what little air I could inhale.

My bladder let go as the wraith wailed. Urine pooled beneath me, dripped to the floor, ran down my legs, and dampened my socks. The depths of her empty sockets flashed red fire as she shrieked. That arm never wavered in its quest, did not lower or twist. It pointed exactly as she had in the backyard. Thunder clapped overhead, ripping me from my paralysis.

I bolted to my feet, scrambling in fright away from

the specter as she dissipated in a gust of gray mist. I stood in shock at the library door. My heart was galloping in my chest, slamming against my breast-bone as I fought to remain upright. My vision grayed and swirled, grayed and faded, blinking in and out of reality as I swallowed back the bile that threatened to erupt from my throat.Her message was clear. I needed to follow her command.

Empathy and compassion outweighed my fear. If I did not help her? If I could not free her from the bonds that held her here, who would or could? Trembling but resolved on the matter, I shuffled back into the library, scooped the journal from the chaise, grateful that the evidence of my fright had not yet seeped into the journal, then picked up the candle.

Taking a moment to steady my nerves, I closed my eyes, inhaled deeply, then released it. A minute later, I spoke into the silence.

"Show me."

CHAPTER SIX

I WATCHED THE FIGURE glide across the room and disappear through the wall. Picking up my cell and a candle, I slowly followed. Terror made my insides clench and twist, and my hands shook. I reached the wall she had vanished through and peered out the bank of windows. There she stood, bathed in a beam of moonlight, arm raised, eyes on me. She beckoned. I nodded and turned from the windows. Hopefully she was a patient spirit, as I had to make my way across the library, down the hall, into the kitchen and exit from the enclosed porch. I moved quickly, before logic and sense could redirect my actions.

The candle flickered as I walked through the silent house but held. Entering the kitchen, I moved toward the back door, opened it, and braced myself for the screaming wind and rain. Zipping my jacket a little closer to my neck, I said a silent prayer and opened the porch door. She waited, almost as she had been before, only moved enough for me to see her from where I stood. Her eyes glittered like red jewels in the darkness. Swallowing back fear, I trudged down the steps and walked toward her. My stomach churned and deeper in my gut. I felt my bowels grow watery. My gut cramped and my muscles tightened. My breathing quickened as I grew nearer.

Fear held me in its embrace. Gone was my empathy and my compassion and my curiosity about what had been. I only wanted to go back, to go home, to start this whole day over. Normal people did not follow ghosts into a rainstorm. Hell, normal people don't follow ghosts at all! My brain uttered a string of logic at me, each fact more urgent and hysterical than the last. I stopped mere feet from her, trembling. Rain pelted my face, masking the tears of terror that filled them. Inhale. I held it. Staring at the candle, not at the wraith that stood before me. Exhale. I breathed out. I lifted my eyes.

The twin flames of her misery bore into my soul. She pointed, finger extended, and glided back from me a few paces. She seemed to understand my hesitation in coming closer to her. The wind shrieked around us, but not a hair on her head or a strand of her mourning dress fluttered. She may as well not have been there at all. I could vaguely see the fence behind her, through her. Filaments of moonlight glittered within her shape, making her seem ethereal and beautiful, even in her sorry state of existence.

I focused my eyes on where she pointed, just beyond the trees, and moved once more. I forced myself to remember the passages I had read. Her utter despair and misery. Her grief and sorrow. Her children. Her loneliness. I allowed her words to fuel me as I moved toward the skeletal bowing trees, ancient butlers ready to serve as I approached. My only need was to hear their secrets, to discover what lay within their shadows, buried beneath a carpet of rot and decay. The wind howled. Rain sheeted down from the heavens, torrential and cold. She moved with me, staying away but close enough to remain in my sight. That arm held steady, pointing where I walked.

My candle should have gone out by now, the weak shelter of my cupped palm barely adequate, but my mind accepted that things here were not following the normal rules of reality, at least, not at this current moment in time. I trudged on, feet sinking into soft earth, mud oozing up around the sides of my shoes. Branches snapped under my step. Leaves glittered wetly in the shadows as I made my way along what remained of the path. Set between the ancient oaks, I walked, the lady ever-present in my eyesight. It was unnerving. The most surreal experience of my life and my brain asked me for the thousandth time if we were awake or dreaming or utterly insane.

Minutes passed as I pressed on, deeper into the back of the estate and suddenly, as lightning lit the sky overhead, the trees gave way to a clearing. What had once been a pleasant grove for picnics was now an overgrown nightmare of twisted vines, drooping bushes, creeping ivy and shrubs that clung to the stone benches and spiraled around the bases of the statues that stood guard. The lady moved once more as I stopped, flickering in and out of existence, much like my candle. Seconds later, she stood over a spot a scant five yards from me. The rusted remains of an old water pump were sticking out of the ground like a morbid reminder of what lay beneath.

I jumped, startled, as thunder rolled across the sky. Wind whipped my hair around me, stinging my cheeks. Rain had soaked me to the bone, and I shivered, both from the cold and the fear that was consuming me. I moved toward her, terrified to face her wrath again. She glided away by inches as I came nearer, keeping space between us. As I reached the spot she vacated, I peered down at the ground. A square door was set into the ground, much like a trapdoor would be in a basement.

I set the candle down on the bench nearby and bent to the door. The handle felt icy and slick in my hand. Flecks of metal flaked off in my hand as I gripped it and pulled. Hope told me that maybe it wouldn't open, but my brain chortled insanely as soon as I had the thought. Of course, it would open. She would make it open. I knew that as well as I knew my own name. A grating noise emitted from the rusted hinges, almost frozen shut with age, cold, and rusted rot. I adjusted my grip and pulled it again. It rose. A fetid stench wafted from the pit, assaulting me. I dropped the lid in surprise, gasping for breath. I staggered backwards, bile rising in my throat. My eyes stung and my mouth opened, drawing in great gulps of air.

She moved closer, pointing. Those eyes glittered redder, darker, angrier. She moved again, finger pointing at the lid. I trembled. Took a breath and steadied myself the best I could and bent to the task again. This time, I held my breath and pulled hard, rising with the lid as it rose from the ground. An earthen pit met my stare. A ladder was bolted to the sides. Terror roiled within me. I knew without a doubt that I would need to go down there. This would not end until I did this task for her. Whatever she needed me to see was down there in the dark, rotting and decaying and screaming for peace. I stared at her. Her eyes were locked on the well now, a deep sorrow on her sunken face. Her gaze lifted to mine. I sighed and lifted my candle.

MY HEART DROPPED INTO the pit of my stomach as I peered into the dank dark of the pit before me. Vines, roots, and webs reach up the sides, woven around the ladder, and stretched across the hole as far as I could see. I wanted to vomit, but more so, I wanted to flee. I wanted to run from here, run into the woods, into the street, anywhere but here. I knew I could not. My heart kept me here, kept me invested. I had to help her. I had to see this through, somehow.

The fetid stench still wafted from below, clinging to my skin like a wet blanket. The storm had cleansed the worst of it away, but I knew as I descended, it would thicken like a fog borne of decay and rot and death. I saw her drifting closer to me, fury creeping across her face; directed at me or triggered by the memory she was reliving. I had no way of knowing. I turned, set the candle down beneath the stone bench and popped my cell phone into my teeth, flashlight on, camera end sticking out like a crazy lollipop. I knelt on the soggy ground and twisted my body around, dangling my feet into the well, searching for purchase on the ladder. I found it, heaved a sigh around the device in my mouth, and descended.

Her blazing eyes locked onto mine as I stared upward, desperately clinging to the moonlight as I went deeper into the sodden earth. Her features were barely visible as I went lower, but those sunken eyes followed my every move. Red flickers like flames pierced the darkness beyond my reach, seeking whatever lies beneath me. The iron was slick in my grip, wet from the drenching rain, scratchy and coarse from flaking rust and age. I moved at a snail's pace, breathing heavily, drool slipping from the edges of my mouth from clenching my phone between my teeth.

Step down. Step down. Adjust my hold on the ladder.

Breathe in. Breathe out. Step down. Step down.

Again. I focused on the process. I brought my eyes to stare at the dirt before me, not the lady, not the webs clinging to my cheeks or the vines scratching my ankles.

Step down. Step down. Adjust. Inhale. Exhale. Again.

Eternity passed before my feet sank into sodden ground. The scent of death coated my tongue, drifted down my lungs, filled my chest with its heavy decay. Earthy and old, it brought a heavy dose of sadness to my heart as I steeled myself to turn around and see what the Lady wanted me to see. I removed the phone from my mouth, adjusted the light to the highest brightness I could get, and turned.

Here, at the bottom of the well, wrapped in tattered cloth and twisted vines and roots, lay a body. Tufts of hair still clung to the skeletal skull that lie askew from the neck, broken in the fall, if I had to guess. The barest remnants of sinew held the bones together within what remained of the clothing. Water and time had wreaked havoc upon the corpse as it had lain here for decades, submerged in inches of water and mud. A thick sludge of silt and insects oozed from the crevices that my light fell across. The body was male if the clothing was a sign. Grayed bits of flesh still showed beneath a ruined shirt, a suit vest, and trousers. A pair of rotted boots were near the feet: long ago fallen away as the rats and mice and bugs had their fill of blood and flesh.

I glanced up, seeing nothing but those red flickers in the dark, but I could hear her. The sudden wail of despair, a shriek so mournful and sorrowful that I shuddered. I heard her in my head, like she was right beside me, inside me, behind me. The cry echoed around me, reverberated around the pit, pierced the night like a gunshot. When it ended, I inhaled sharply, almost gasping for air as the sound released me from its captivity. I squatted closer to the body, seeing something more in the dim light of my phone. A bundle of rags lie near the right arm, what looked to be blankets, baby blankets.

My blood ran cold. I stared at the remnants. What had been delicate lace edges were now ruined edges of aged, desiccated cotton. I looked up again, seeing the pinpoints, but no wailing came. She waited. I knew she was waiting. I reached a hand out and tugged the cloth away. The smallest fragment of a bone showed, then became a tiny arm reaching toward the sky, then another. When the minuscule skull rolled toward me with its empty eyes, it broke me and I backpedaled, scrabbling away on my ass in the mud.

Horrified, I could only stare at what had been a baby, down here in the arms of who? Jonathan, I had assumed, but the baby was too tiny to be one of the daughters. *Who then? What baby?* I stared upward into the night, appalled and terrified.

Had she done this? Or had Jonathan tried to flee with the baby in his arms and fell to his death? Questions flooded my brain as tears sluiced down my cheeks, blending with the cold rain. I heard the wail this time, further away, drifting from above. This one full of sorrow, pain, and maybe regret? It hurt to hear it. I wanted to comfort her, but how does one comfort a ghost? One that most likely had harmed another, or possibly killed.

THE WAILING CONTINUED. IT raked across my skull, seeped into my bones, and chilled me to my core. Something dark fell across the opening of the well and I looked up, terror freezing me in place as a pale, wispy shape floated toward me from above. I scrabbled backward even more, pressing my body against the cold dirt of the earthen walls. Seconds later, it fluttered to a stop at my feet. A sheet. A moth-eaten, once cream-colored sheet lies over the tangles of vines and roots, resting just atop the baby's corpse. I looked at it, confused for a moment before she spoke, more of a whisper that I heard in my head rather than with my ears.

Bring her.

Shivering but not able to deny the request, I gingerly retrieved the cloth from the ground and shuffled over to the miniscule remains of the infant. Trying to remember that this was once a baby, an innocent thing of hope and humanity, I knelt beside it and gently picked up the body, setting it on the sheet. I searched through the rags and found all the pieces I could and finished by laying the pitiful skull on top of its bones. Then I wrapped the bundle into a closed swaddle, much like one would a baby, except this one was not cooing and blinking at me from the opening. There was no need for an opening on this bundle. Finished, I stood and tucked it close against me, staring at what remained of Jonathan.

Feeling foolish but compelled to do so, I said a quick but silent prayer for his soul, bent down to cover the body the best I could with the rags that were left, then I turned to the ladder. She waited just at the top; I could see the lace of her skirts, the mud that clung to them, the ivy, and the dead leaf fragments glistening wetly from the storm. I began the ascent, keeping my head down, blinking away the raindrops that pattered against my face.

When I reached the top, I set the bundle down, crawled over the edge of the well and replaced the cover. The lady hovered a few feet away, no longer wailing, but her eyes glimmered with the deep red flashes, staring directly at me, watching my every move. I stood and lifted the baby once more, waiting to see what would come next. Some of my terror had faded, but I was no longer sure if I was safe in this pursuit or not. Too late to consider that now. She began to move, turning to beckon me with one long finger. I sighed and followed, cursing my tender heart all the while.

She led me to the house, back to the library, to the chaise where I had my things and her diary. She pointed at the aged leather book. I stared, not sure I understood. The bundle in my arms was tragically light but heavy in its reminder that I held a deceased baby. Those eyes flashed with insistence or anger. I couldn't be sure which, but I sat on the chaise and laid the bundle beside me. As I picked up the book, the lady moved away to her corner, almost vanishing into the shadowy corner. I could feel her presence lingering as I moved to the next page of the journal. Clearly, there was something more I was to read. I began.

CHAPTER SEVEN

Oak Helm Manor–January 28, 1921

I HOPE MOTHER AND Father both are rotting in shallow graves wherever they may be across the seas. In some wretched pit of hell and despair, writhing in eternal agony as the flames of Satan sear the flesh from their bones. How does one fail their child so? How is this allowed in polite society to not prepare your child for life beyond the nursery, beyond the nanny and the classroom? Death is seen from afar, with a chaste hug, a pat on the head, and off to bed with a cup of tea and a biscuit.

It's a polite sadness, not truly felt, not truly seen. It's spoken of in hushed whispers with the pastor and

Missus Jacobs from Wickingham Lane. Its mother quietly crying behind closed doors and delicate lace handkerchiefs; its father, stoic and stern, next to a wooden box that holds his father. Eyes dark, brow furrowed, a nod and a handshake as businessmen pass by to stare upon the cold face contained within the box.

What is this wretched living pain that I am living with? That roils within me like a caged beast that is slowly tearing free, one claw through my heart at a time? This cannot be normal. This pain. This ache that grips my body, my very heart, and the soul which yearns for comfort, for a kindness, for death or mercy or anything outside of this pain that consumes me. How does one live with this? How do you breathe the air again? How do you walk in the daylight or feel the sunshine on your face without crumbling into grief upon the pathway?

Food has no taste. The tea is always weak, always dull. I eat because I must, when I remember I must. The bread is stale. The milk is always gone bad. I barely remember when the milkman delivers. Often, I go days without opening the door, only to find the crate of bottles staring accusingly at me, curdled in the sun. There's no meat left. No vegetables from the garden. I care naught. Jonathan stays away for days at a time. I don't speak at all anymore; I fear that I no longer know how. My voice only cracks and ripples into loud, angry sobs when I try to form words. Or venom passes through my teeth every time I see his weary face. His sunken eyes and pale skin, the scruff of his whiskers keeping him partly in shadow, like a walking demon.

I loathe his presence. I curse myself for ever having felt love for this man. For this vile disgrace of hurt and abuse, for this adulterer that shares my bed. I feel his weight beside me at night. He sneaks in like a thief, long after the lamps have burned out. He lies beside me, and I can feel the words hovering in the air above our heads. Words that he cannot say, lies that I will not hear. I rise after his snores fill the room and I retreat to my hallways, walking and pacing and crying silent tears once more, tears that of late have been borne of hate, of anger, of all-consuming pain.

Today, though, the worst of all the things, the insult that I can no longer ignore, can no longer bear. She returned with a driver guiding her to our door. She is kneeling, gushing blood, doubled over in pain. The child comes. Their child. He lets her in, guides her to our marriage bed, not her cold garret room, but to our marriage bed, and bids her rest. He sends the driver for the doctor in town and all but shrieks at me to help.

What am I to do? I am no midwife, nor do I care to ease her woes. I simply stare at her body, sweating and twisting on my bed, her blood staining my sheets. Their sin seeping from between her legs. The baby demands entry. I refuse. I watch. She screams and begs. She pushes. I do nothing. I feel nothing but hate. I relish her pain.

Jonathan rushes in, doctor in tow. I am still standing, merely watching from the corner as he turns on me, slapping me so hard my teeth burst through my lip, and I grin like a fiend and say nothing. I watch her bleed on my bed. I watch the doctor try to aid her. I watch Jonathan trip over himself to try to be useful and he is not. The babe comes, pathetic and pale, bloody and wailing; it's a girl.

My heart stutters. My soul clings to the only madness that is left. It is a girl, my daughter, brought back to me. I blink and see the eyes. My Lilah's eyes. My daisy girl, my sweet, sweet flower girl, my Lilah has returned. I rise to my feet and reach for her, my paralysis broken, my need too great. My daughter has returned. I take her from the doctor, tears in my eyes. She is mine. She is back. Jonathan is screaming, but I hear no words. I only stare at my daughter's face, cloaked in this new one.

I PUT THE JOURNAL down, overwhelmed by the words. There is so much anguish and despair within. The pain clenches within my heart, stabs deep into my gut. So much hurt and loss. The lady lingers on the edge of my vision, wringing her hands as she watches me. Those eyes are darker, less flamelike and more of a glassy red, like stained glass orbs staring at me.

Pain. I can see it on the haunted countenance of her face. I feel pity now.

Madness consumed her. Insanity brought on by despair. The baby, the illegitimate child of the nanny, and Jonathan. The bundle to my left, all that remained. I looked at it, then back at the shrouded specter in the corner. She took the child for her own. But what then?

I jumped, shrieking slightly as a massive clap of thunder echoed over the house. When I recovered from the shock, she was closer, hovering in front of the fireplace, pointing at the book. There was more. This I knew already. There must be so much more. What happened the night Jonathan ended up in the well and how or why was the baby with him there? Questions filled me. I nodded at her, just once, and reached for the book again.

Oak Helm Manor-February 15, 1921

THE BABE IS HUNGRY. *She squirms in my arms, delicate pink limbs reaching from her blankets. Her face wrinkles up and her mouth opens, ready to cry out for food. I watch her, love all but radiating from my body. I vibrate from within, every fiber of my soul glow-*

ing with adoration. Her every movement is magical, every sound is melodic, like tinkering wind chimes in the morning sun. The downy hair on her head is wispy, daisy yellow. She will be blond like my Lilah, this new Lilah of mine. I call her the same. Why else would I call her by any other name? She is my Lilah, mine, not theirs. Not the seed of sin, but a gift sent back from heaven. An angel given back to me to ease my suffering. Who am I to argue with the Lord?

Jonathan waits on his harlot day and night as she wastes away in our bed. The blood still flows from within her. The doctor can no longer help. He only shakes his head, whispers somber words and slinks away with his money clutched in his wrinkled fist. I sneer as he departs, my Lilah in my arms. I don't need him, or Jonathan, and I certainly don't need his whore. All that I need is this miracle in my arms.

I enter the room, refusing to meet his eyes as he watches me from the corner. She wakes, reaches for her, weakly, skin almost yellow, eyes sunken. She offers a smile. I refuse to see it. I hand my daughter over, gently, and order her to nurse. She whispers 'Thank you' as if I am offering her a kindness. I can feel my lips twist in a sneer. She is naught to me but a dairy cow, a sickly one at that.

I can no longer nurse. Jonathan refuses to leave the house to fetch a goat. As long as her heart beats, my Lilah will feed from the wretch that birthed her. I am too hesitant to try regular milk yet, but perhaps soon. My young Lilah is far too delicate, too tender, to fill her insides with such richness. I stand at the foot of the bed, watching, pondering upon when to introduce more milk into my deliveries from the milkman as I watch Lilah latch on to the woman in my bed. I see the smile on her face, half-buried beneath the shadows, and my insides twist.

Let her smile. Let her have these moments. Lilah is mine. She was only the vessel. I will do what I must to keep her fed and healthy. Soon my use of these vile two humans will be done, then I'll decide what to do. For now, Lilah eats. Her tiny gasps as she suckles fills my heart with the upmost joy. I watch, staring at her face, her dark eyes so much like mine. Her tiny fists grasp at the edge of the blanket. The whore lifts a finger to caress the babe's cheek and I clear my throat, a warning sound. She stops, her eyes meeting mine. She drops her hand back down, choosing instead to draw the child closer to her breast. The only touch I'll allow her.

Jonathan shifts in his seat. I can smell his odor from here. I glare at him.

"Go clean yourself. You reek of filth and piss." I order. He barely lifts his gaze to mine, but stands and shuffles away to the bathroom. He knows I'll only allow his absence until Lilah is finished with her feeding. I'll not linger here in this death chamber. I'll not be her maid, nor his. He cooks for her. He cleans her with warm towels. I hear him trudging along the hallways and the stairs late at night when he thinks I am asleep. I am not. I am watching, always watching

from the corners. Lilah in my arms, we walk the halls. I hold her. I sing to her. And I plan their demise. I will keep her safe, no matter the cost. They will not take her from me.

The woman shifts Lilah from her breast and wraps her blankets tighter around her. Sadness fills her expression as she begins to lift her, but I'm already there, taking my daughter from her, setting her on my shoulder to pat her back. I don't even acknowledge the broken woman reclining in my bed. She is food, a warm bottle, nothing more. Blood drips to the floor from beneath the blankets, a steady pool seeping into the wood. I ignore it. She is his problem, not mine.

I hear his footsteps and turn as he shuffles back into the room. Wrinkled but clean clothes cover his frame. The stench is gone, but the stubble remains on his gaunt face, like an ever-expanding death mask, taking over one day at a time. Lilah coos and I settle her in my arms.

He speaks, his voice a raspy whisper in the quiet room.

"Please order from the butcher today. There's no meat, no broth. Milk and eggs too. She weakens…"

I shoot him a glare, and he stops speaking. I don't care what she is doing or feeling. I nod once and leave the room as more blood splatters on the floor. I'll order food, the poorest cuts that I can. I do not care how it tastes. I only need to keep her alive a little while longer, not fed with veal and lamb.

Lilah coos again, and I descend the stairs, ignoring the sob that follows my departure. I spend my days in the library and the atrium, Lilah in my arms, faded songs fall my from lips, humming tunes I no longer remember, nursery rhymes that no longer hold their cadence. Nonsense words to fill the silence as Lilah slumbers in my arms.

I CLOSED THE JOURNAL and stared at the shadows, seeing the sweep of her skirts, the wisps of her hair over her shoulders. The lady had retreated to the window and was staring outside. The storm had quieted, passing over now, though rain still fell in a steady curtain. I wasn't sure if I should feel pity or horror. All that she had endured. A lady, that I imagined, had once been elegant and dignified; the lady of the manor, hosting parties and running the household, doting on her daughters, only to have this misery placed upon her shoulders. Betrayal and sorrow, hurt and distrust, her life brought to ruin at the hands of the man that was to love and protect her.

It was tragic. The things people do to one another, the evil we bring to those we love from our own weakness, from cowardice and greed. Contempt for her husband filled me then, a deep loathing of my own for all that she had endured. It was no wonder that madness had gripped her, amplified by her grief and pain. Her words from the journal lingered in my heart. How does one endure so much without losing themselves along the way?

She turned from the window, gliding across the room. My eyes tracked her movements to the far side where she lingered. When she lifted her head, those eyes flashed at me, red flickers in the dim candlelight. I followed her arm as it moved. Next to her, a cradle stood not quite waist-high, filmed in strands of cobwebs and dust, partially hidden by the draperies. I didn't need her to speak to understand what she wanted.

I rose from the couch and lifted the bundle of bones and blankets. Holding it close to my chest, I carried it to her and placed the remains in the cradle. A long sigh whispered through the room, vibrating with such deep sorrow that it hurt my heart. She still loved the babe, all that remained of her life that once was. A reminder of what she once had, what was taken, and what she still yearned for. A tear rolled from my eye as I watched her stand over the cradle. A haunting tune filled the room then, and a chill ran down my spine.

CHAPTER EIGHT

Oak Helm Manor–February 28, 1921

THE WHORE IS DEAD. *Passed in the night while Jonathan kept his pathetic vigil at her side. Blood has clotted beneath my bed, tacky and browning. Thick smears of it run down the sides, staining the mahogany, all of it ruined. The bedsheets soaked with it. My marriage quilt, hand-trimmed in satin, now a funeral shroud. Things my mother spent months sewing for my hope chest, things meant for a happy bride and a well-appointed boudoir for her groom. Now rot beneath his whore's corpse, stained beyond what any amount of laundering could ever do. My mother is no longer here to replace these things, and what of me?*

What about that which I have lost? Who is going to replace me? I am broken to pieces, shattered glass held together by thread and corsets, a haunt in my own halls. A ghost, a specter, a shadow of grief and hate, rage and sorrow. So much more pain than anyone ever warned of. My fairy tale books shed no light on such matters when I was a child reading by mother's knee. Barely thirty years on this earth and my husband is a vile adulterer, my daughters are dead, cold and alone in the ground and I am naught but a ghost roaming this manor that stands more silent than any mausoleum ever has. At least those cold marble structures house insects and rats that skitter and scurry among the dead leaves and dry bones. The only rat here wears my husband's face.

He came to me last night for solace, seeking comfort of some kind, falling upon his knees in the library where I slept, as Lilah slumbered in her cradle nearby. His tear-stained face dropping to my breast. His skeletal arms wrapping my neck in his grief-stricken state. Wails shook him as I pushed away. Wails and cries and sobs that I was ordered to silence upon seeing him fucking that trollop in her attic bed. I pushed him to the floor, sitting up with nary a word, and left the room, Lilah in my arms. He would find no comfort here, not from my daughter or I. I left him wailing on his knees.

There was nothing for him here, not anymore. There is no forgiveness. No wife waiting for his em-

brace. There is only Lilah and I. We will be all we need. Her and I and the manor. I've given him a list of demands he is to meet. I care naught where he goes so long as he provides for the manor and my child. I will keep his secrets as long as our needs are met. I cannot look at him any longer. Every second he lingers here, drives my blood into a boiling frenzy, a seething hate.

Only Lilah's darling face calms the storm in my heart, the only bliss in my mournful life. The rose of her cheeks, the softness of her hair, the eyes that watch mine as she smiles and coos in my arms. She is all I need to move on from this. I will be a mother again. I will be the lady of the manor once more and she will be endlessly adored.

TEARS POUR DOWN MY cheeks when I pause in my reading. The sadness is too much. Her anguish and despair, too visceral; the pain on every page like a steel blade in my chest. I thought I had problems. My silly teen girl problems were minor annoyances compared to this poor soul hovering in the shadows.

I turned to her from where I sat, watching the rain pelt the windows, seeing the final streaks of lightning color the sky with bruised purples and blues as the storm moved slowly on. I wondered idly about my role in this night.

Was I meant to be here? Did I cause her to appear? Did she wander here nightly, just waiting for someone to stumble inside? Or was I chosen? Did she know I would help her? Was I connected somehow to this sad tale?

I sensed a change in the air, a heaviness that chilled my flesh, a deep sorrow that settled over me like a wet blanket. I looked at her to see her gazing at me, almost through me as I mused on the events of the night. I didn't know what more was to come, but I knew I would help put her to rest. I would see this story through. Fear was no longer an excuse or a deterrent. I knew she would not harm me; she was only ever seeking help, nothing more.

I waited silently, watching as she glided from the window, passing the desk and the fireplace, then hovering in the doorway, waiting. Her arm lifted, the finger extended, her head cocked to one side. I nodded and followed the grieving specter from the room, taking the candle from the table as I passed. There was something more I had to do.

I FOLLOWED THE LADY from the house into the early morning haze. A gauzy mist clung to everything, fat droplets of rain hung heavy from leaves and branches and shimmered on cobwebs in the dying hedges. I shivered as the chill in the air rippled my flesh, causing goosebumps to cover my arms and neck. The candle in my hand flickered but remained lit. Not knowing where I was being led, I was hesitant to put it down. She glided over the dew-laden grass, hovering just inches over the stone pathway as she moved toward the fountain near the back of the property.

Stone benches lined the perimeter of the algae-slick basin. Gargoyles and one-eyed fish were carved into the marble. The spouts were ringed with a rust-colored tinge, the only evidence of the water that had once gushed forth. The benches sat atop the same stones that matched the pathway. Flat stones with a hint of beige, gold, and gray running through them.

I gazed around the fountain, trying to see how it may have looked when lush with life and filled with sparking, clean water, fish, and flowers. The small grove it sat within was quite lovely; a sanctuary meant to relax in, perhaps read a book or have a tea party with your daughters. My heart ached for her. I could almost see them there, laughing and playing beneath her doting eye.

She had stopped moving and stood waiting by the bench on the far side. Her eyes found mine, that flickering red gaze. I padded over near her, not sure what I was meant to do yet. Setting the candle down on the bench, I looked where she pointed at the ground. Weeds split the stone beneath our feet. Ivy tendrils crept over the fountain, winding and weaving among and carvings.

The lady moved slightly. Her eyes flashed when

I looked up and that arm gestured to her feet once more. I still saw nothing but moved closer still. She backed away, keeping to our unspoken agreement of space maintained between us. Squatting, I saw the bigger of the stones beneath the bench were cracked more than the rest, deep splits cutting it in two. The others next to it were the same. Reaching a hand down, I wiped the muddy grime from the area, searching for something more, another clue for what I was to do. Fingers dug into the mud between the stones. I pulled it, struggling to lift the weight but slowly it budged, a wet sucking sound emitted as the rain-soaked ground released its hold. A wooden slat could be seen beneath. I understood what I was to do. Whatever I needed to see was beneath that wood, hidden in the dirt.

I knelt fully on the ground, digging into the ground, tugging the stone pieces up one by one. The wood became clearer, fully visible beneath a layer of dirt, wriggling worms, and scuttling beetles. My only problem now was the bench itself. It looked to be heavy, carved from the same marble as the fountain. Moving it would be impossible. I looked at it, took a shot, and leaned into it, pushing with all I had. It rocked backwards an inch, but dropped into place once more.

I would need something, a tool or a solid branch, something to use like a lever. Rising from the ground, I brushed the debris from my knees and looked around. The lady looked impatient but watched silently. Walking toward the hedgerow, I kept my eyes peeled on the ground for anything usable. A thick branch stuck out a few feet away, and I stooped down to grab it. Huffing in frustration when I saw that it was only a few inches long, I tossed it back.

Movement caught my eye again, and I turned. The lady was hovering by my shoulder, her visage glitching in that odd way it did when she roamed too far from the manor. She was pointing again. I wanted to mutter something unkind about her impatience, but then I saw where she pointed. Further along the bushes, near the fence line, several long shapes were visible beneath the tendrils of ivy.

I nodded and shuffled over, trying not to slip on the overgrown vines that wove all over the area. Dead bushes, shrubs, and trees lined the pathways and fence line. The ivy had taken over, crawling over everything, up and around and across. Silken spiderwebs glistened in the shadowy corners, with the owners perched warily in the middle, watching me with tiny beady eyes. My skin crawled as I reached for the handle of the rusted spade that lay discarded at the fence.

Turning, I went to the bench where the lady waited and looked at my dilemma once more. If I could get the bench lifted another inch or two, I could slide the spade beneath and use the handle to lever it back while I pushed it. It sounded possible, but what the hell did I know? I shrugged and knelt again. I took a deep breath and readied myself, then shoved the bench with my chest and shoulders and one hand, gripping the spade in the other. As soon as I saw the legs lift the slightest, I shoved the rusted tool into it.

Taking another breath, I heaved again, pushing the bench once more and slid the tool deeper beneath the leg. Standing, I glanced over and spoke to the lady, "I hope this works." Then I planted one foot on the handle and used my other knee and both hands to push against the bench. It rocked back, and I gave a final heave with a sudden shout, ramming my body against it. It fell over, slamming into the stone behind it with a crash. Even the lady looked startled at the noise it made, so loud it was in the silent morning.

In its place, long wooden slats were visible. Four of them laid into the ground. I shuddered and my stomach clenched, already in knots. I could smell the stench of ancient death from where I stood. I was eager to get this over with now. It had been a long, creepy night. The sun would be up soon, and I wanted to go home. My body hurt. My heart and my mind hurt for all that had happened here in this manor, and I felt so terrible for this poor soul trapped here. I knew I couldn't leave without trying to help ease her burden, somehow.

I got back on the ground and began to yank the boards away, gasping as the foul stench of skeletal rot drifted from the earth. One by one, the boards left the ground with a squelch. Mud clung to the undersides; worms wriggled from view. And there, as I moved the last slat, there she was. A skeleton with long hair still atop the skull. The rictus grin staring at the sky.

The legs twisted in a heap, as if no care was taken with how the body was laid. The arms were on each side; the skull turned horribly too far to the left as if the neck had been broken to fit the body into the space allowed. Tatters of blankets clung to the frame and poked out from beneath. Satin lined, damp and full of holes, the bones lay in a jumbled, forced heap in its shallow grave. It could only be the nanny.

I looked at the lady then, not shocked at all. I think I knew what I would find. None of them had ever left this manor. The events of the diary were not yet over. The bond keeping her here was not yet broken. Not waiting for instructions, I leaned into the earth and began to tug the rotten fabric up, keeping the bones contained within the best I could.

Behind me, I heard the lady sigh. A deep aching sigh from within her core, full of sorrow and pain. That single sound said more in that moment than her diary ever could.

Oak Helm Manor–March 3, 1921

MADNESS HAS TAKEN OVER the manor. Jonathan is not himself. I am not sure that I am myself, not anymore.

I barely recognize myself in the mirror. The creature that stares back at me is a skeletal façade of the girl I was once, pale, gaunt, haunted by things that should never have been. Jonathan stalks the manor, muttering to himself. He is unkempt and dirty. He does not eat. He does not sleep. I can feel him watching me at all hours. He waits for me to sleep, to put Lilah down, but I shall not. I will not let him have her. He took everything from me. He will NOT take her too.

*I walk the upper halls, cradling her to my breast, singing lullabies and stroking her back. Breathing in her scent, that perfume that only babies seem to have, it's everything to me. That aroma that speaks of hope, of new life, of the memories of my own babes in my arms, my other daughters as they once were. He **cannot** have her. I can feel my sanity slipping as days of not sleeping weigh my body and my mind down. Shadows move just beyond my vision. Noises abound at all hours of the night, creaks and cries and groans. Fingers of bone tap on the windows and scratch at the floorboards as I walk both day and night.*

Jonathan sneaks about when I fall quiet. I can hear his shoddy footsteps, barely upright as he shuffles along the floor and up the stairs. He is searching, always searching. It's become a game of cat and mouse, of endless hide and seek. Up he comes, down the back stairs I go. Down he shuffles. Back up I go, to the attic, to the windows in the turrets where I gaze down upon my beloved fountain. Exhaustion drags at my feet, slowing my gait, making my steps every bit as unbalanced as Jonathan's, but I will not submit.

He screams for me now. Loud roars echo in the silent rooms. He is angry, raging like a beast. Lilah scrunches her face up to wail, and I soothe her, walking, walking, walking away. Up the stairs, around to the back stairs, back down to the kitchen. He pursues, shouting curses all the way.

This is madness. The whore rots in my bed. The doctor has not come to fetch her. The stench is foul, invading every room in the upper hall. Soon I will smell her throughout the entire manor.

Jonathan is quiet now. A door slams. The windows rattle. I stand by the windows in the attic, watching my fountain when he appears. He is holding something, a bundle of rags, something drags by his feet. I peer closer, wiping the misty haze from the glass. He's got the nanny in his arms, his dead rotting whore, wrapped in my bedsheets, held in his arms. I sneer, anger rippling up my spine and scratching at my skull like a thousand angry bees.

Watching him as I rock Lilah against me, I stand at the window to see what the monster does next. He sets his bundle down on the ground next to my fountain and vanishes from my view. When he appears again, he holds the gardener's spade in one hand. At the edge of the pathway, closest to my favorite bench, he starts digging as the gray sky opens overhead, pouring cold rain upon him. My heart seizes in my chest. The final wound to my already broken heart. He means to bury her in my sanctuary, next *to my daughters, in the only place on these wretched grounds that soothes my shattered soul, the only place that I still could claim as my own.*

It is too much to bear. I turn from the window, shaking in rage. This ends now. Fury turns my blood to ice water in my very veins as I storm down the stairs. Stopping in the library to wrap Lilah in her blankets, I set her in her cradle so I can end this insanity once and for all. I will stop him. I will NOT allow this injustice. Lilah whimpers only once as I settle her. Then I turn from the library and stalk toward the kitchen doors, pausing to grab the cleaver from the counter as I pass.

Red clouds my vision. Thunder booms overhead as I step outside. Freezing rain pours down in sheets of gray. I forge ahead, my prey straight ahead, digging in mud, crying out for his whore. He will die where he stands, mark my words. This ends today.

SHAKING, I STOPPED READING for a moment. Too much to process, too much anguish to understand. I stare at the wraith by the window, watch her gazing down at the tiny bundle in the cradle. Her eyes flicker to me, barely registering my presence before she looks at Lilah again. There is more to read, but I don't know if I can. Did she kill him that night? Was the lady a murderer? This was vengeance.

Cold and calculated intent was clearly spelled out in her words. Jonathan had not intended for the first Lilah to die. Her death had been an accident caused by no more than a lazy father and a child's curiosity. The affair was terrible, as it would be for any woman of today to endure, but did that mean one deserved to die? To have their child stolen from them? I wondered which of them had gone mad first, Jonathan or the Lady?

Neither had slept in days, according to her words. Confined to the manor, trapped in this game of hide of seek, relentless in their pursuit of what they wanted, with neither gaining anything in the end but sorrow. It was no wonder that she was burdened to linger here, still seeking the babe, seeking absolution in some way for what had transpired. It hurt. The depths of her pain hurt my heart.

The sorrow I imagine Jonathan felt tugged at my soul. His daughters were gone, his wife turned cold and aloof, the nanny his only comfort dead giving birth to their daughter, only to have her stolen from his very arms. I ached for them both, a tragedy of their own doing. I shook my head and turned back to the diary. I had to finish, for my salvation, if not theirs.

I began to read once more, scooting closer to the flickering candlelight. The words the Lady had scrawled across the page had taken on an angry slant, becoming harder to read on every page.

The pen strokes harsh and ripping, the paper torn through in places as she had scribbled her fury down, underlining words and phrases. Tear stains marred the ink, making the words blotchy but serving to illuminate her pain further.

Oak Helm Manor–March 3, 1921

I SCREAMED HIS NAME as I marched toward him. The wind shrieked it back to me, an echo in the storm. My hair whipped around me, loose and wild, like the anger that guided me. I would endure no more. I would bear witness to his foolish sorrow no longer. HE would leave this house, by force, by my hand, or by his own. Lilah and I would have our peace. I had earned it, sevenfold and sevenfold again. He never looked up as I came toward him. Rage lifted my hand, steeled my heart, cleaver clutched tight, ready to strike.

'Jonathan,' I screamed again, right in his ear. He turned slowly, surprise nowhere on his face, only blind acceptance, a deep pain. The spade fell from his hand, and he backed away a step.

"What is it?" he asked. "What will you have me do? Shall I just lie down and make it easy, or do you

want me to run? What game would suit you best? What penance must I pay now?" He spoke softly. His eyes were cold, almost flat black with exhaustion and pain. There was no light, no spark, not even hate. Just resigned to his fate. I faltered mid-step, cleaver high in hand. My mouth opened, but no sound issued.

Thunder boomed above. Lightning streaked the sky, violet bruises and indigo blue on black. I stared at him, unsure now. He stared back, waiting. I could feel my heart in my throat, pounding in my temple, thrashing like a beast inside my chest.

"Leave." I said, "leave now. Leave your whore. Leave your belongings. Just walk away now and you shall live. I cannot do this any longer. My daughter and I do not need you here."

Something twisted in his face at my words. A bitter expression cut his lips into a snarl. His eyes sparked to life then, cutting through me deeper than any knife ever would.

"My daughter." He spat. "Her name is Bethany, and she is my daughter. Your babes rot there, in the ground at your feet. I will take my leave, my dear. Mark my word. But my daughter is coming with me."

With those words, he stalked off toward the house, leaving me standing there in the storm, his dead mistress at my feet, her blood seeping into the ground where my children rest. Shock froze my limbs and a rush of noise filled my skull like the tearing of parchment from a book. Even the storm did not penetrate my mind as I stood locked in my misery.

I saw him reach the house. I saw him vanish inside. And still, I could not move. Rain sluiced down my face, hiding my tears. The wind tore at my dress, whipping the hem through the mud, billowing it out to brush across the ghastly face of the nanny that I once adored.

A new sound reached my ears. A cry. The wail of a baby. I moved, free of my paralysis. I began to run toward the house. He would not take her from me. Lilah was mine and mine alone! I would kill him first. Time slowed as Jonathan appeared at the back door, a bundle in one arm, his satchel in the other. His eyes pierced me, a heated dagger into my heart, slicing through my bones and into my heart. Hate bloomed fresh in my bosom.

My legs moved faster now. My arms were outstretched. Blood pulsed in my ears as my feet pounded down the pathway. He moved, clutching the babe to his chest, cradling her. He ran. I chased. Thunder crashed and lightning slammed into the earth mere feet from where I stood. He dashed across the grass then, headed for the side gate, into the woods that would lead him to the village road.

My feet turned without thought, my body followed. My brain stuttered inside its cocoon of noise and cotton. Nothing was there but red rage, red, red, red, red pulsed in my mind, in my eyesight. He cut past me. I shrieked and lunged for him, grabbing his coattail as it whipped by my hands. He stumbled. A shout *left his lips. He slid across wet grass but remained upright. Lilah was wailing in his arms. Wailing for me.*

I lunged for her, grasping the blankets, ripping and pulling, trying to free her. Jonathan pushed me away. There was a sudden CRACK, a loud yell, and he fell. They were falling. I blinked rain from my eyes, wiped the mess of my hair from my face in time to see them disappearing into the earth.

The well! That godforsaken well that he was to cover once and for all had swallowed them whole. The wooden cover sat charred and broken in two, smoking from the lightning strike, split in half. Jonathan struck it in his scramble to get away and down they went into the same pit where Lilah had died barely a year before.

I screamed, dropping to my knees, screaming for her, for my Lilah. No sound met my ears save the shrieking of the wind. No babe, no cries for help, no tiny wails of a child in pain. No begging from the man that I had once loved. Silence deafened the storm surging away. Silence overpowered everything. I could not hear my own screaming. I did not feel the blood gush from my ruptured throat. I did not notice the red haze in my eyes from the burst vessels from the agonized shrieks that I surely was issuing. Silence prevailed.

When dawn broke through the skeletal trees around the manor, I pulled myself to the edge of the pit to peer in. Two shapes, broken and bent beneath muddy blankets and thorny vines. I gave no cry. No sound was left within me, no life was left here. This manor was cursed, as was I. I rose from the ground, defeated.

SOBS SHOOK ME AS I set the journal down beside me. Her pain was so great I could only weep in response. I could feel her eyes on me as she stood sentry across the room. A shadow of pain, sorrow, and misery. A ghost caught in her own nightmare, looping through the same storm on repeat, never to be free. She had intent, but the final act had not been her doing, not wholly. Anger and pain had driven them both to acts of insane desperation. The story was almost finished. I could feel it. I wiped my eyes and turned to her, watching her glide closer to the door.

I rose quietly from the chaise, and lifting the candle again, I followed her into darkness.

CHAPTER NINE

OUT INTO THE EARLY morning, we went. A heavy mist hung over the lawn, shimmering in the first strokes of golden sunlight. Following the lady toward the fountain, I could only wonder what my next task may be. The night had been long and devastating, but somehow soothing to my own childish worries over my failed romance. This poor lady that guided me now had suffered so much more at the hands of her loved one that I could only shed tears of the pain I imagined she felt. To feel her pain, the absolute depths of her grief, those were emotions that I did not yet have.

I wanted to help ease her burden somehow and if this night was destined for me, then I would be grateful to be of service. I did not believe in coincidences, everything had a reason for occurring, everything was connected, whether we understood it or not. If my situation led me here, if the storm kept me here, then here is where I was meant to be. The lady chose to show herself to me; she did not have to. Whatever task I was to do, I would do the best I could to bring this tragedy to a more peaceful close.

As she glided to a stop by the fountain, I gazed into the empty eyes. The red flickers seemed dull. The anger was fading from her. I could feel it. Grief was replacing it, filling her with the grip of sorrow as she released the last vestiges of her rage. She shifted, and I followed her gaze downward. The body of the nanny rested at her feet, where I had unearthed her only an hour before. The remains were little more than tatters of garments and brittle bone, soaked through from the heavy downpour.

I watched the lady move away, and I waited. An itch grew in the back of my mind. I think I knew my task but kept still, waiting to be shown. Seconds later, she stopped at the well, hovering just beyond the dark reaches of the pit. She looked at me. I nodded, understanding what I was to do. I bent to the bundle on the ground and lifted it gently into my arms. The remains of the nanny were to be united with Jonathan, where he lay deep in the well.

Trudging through wet grass with the bundle in my arms, I made my way to the pit where the lady stood and set them down. The lady gazed at the remains, hurt and sorrow emanating from her. The reds of her eyes flared, then settled. I could see the internal war being waged. Anger and forgiveness fought for control as she stared at the bones of the mistress and further beyond, the bones of her husband. I felt the sorrow settle within her once more, and she nodded at me, then vanished from my view.

Used to her disappearances, I wasn't disturbed. I knelt on the grass and tried to tie the bundle of cloth and bone into a more secure package that I could carry. After a couple of tries and dealing with wet, muddy and rotted fabric, I managed a tightly wrapped parcel that I could hold with one hand. I shifted my body where I knelt and dangled one foot into the pit, searching for the ladder. I found it and shuffled my body down a step or two until I was fully standing on the rusty steps, then reached for the bundle and brought it with me into the darkness.

I descended carefully, one rung at a time. The stench of decay was not as bad as it had been the first time. Rain and the nighttime air had swept the pit free of it. The earthy scent of mud, soil, and vines met my nostrils instead, and I welcomed it. Less than a minute later, I stepped free of the ladder and set the bundle down next to Jonathan. Not knowing what else to do, I muttered a quick prayer and bade them to rest well in peace and turned back to the ladder.

I climbed from the pit, weary but content with my role in this endeavor. Putting the bodies to rest in their rightful place would surely help the lady find her peace. Maybe now she could be free of this burden and make her own way to the light that waited for her. Thoughts of the lady seemed to summon her as she was suddenly there as my head emerged at the top of the well. My gaze landed on her skirts first, then traveled upward to see her frail arms holding a bundle. Then my eyes went to her gaunt face to find her eyes focused on mine.

I stifled the sigh. My task was not yet done. The baby needed to be with her parents. Bethany, as was her rightful name, needed to be placed with Jonathan and the nanny. This was the final act of the lady. To put the child she had claimed as her own back in the arms of those that created her.

My heart broke for her. To know such sadness, long after death, to carry such guilt with you, decades after your demise, to be trapped in the very place that brought such pain; it was all too much to comprehend. I took the baby as she offered it and began my descent once more. A gentle breeze picked up, sweeping through my wet clothes, and I shuddered. The wail hidden in the wind made the hairs on my neck stand at attention. The lady wept alone in the dawn, waiting for my return.

I made quick work of settling the baby between her parents and tried to arrange them close together as if they were cradling her. The two adult skulls were side by side, with the tiny head of the baby beneath them, a ghastly family portrait If I had ever seen one. Another muttered prayer and a heaving sob from my chest were the final sounds I uttered in the dank pit of death before I ascended once more.

WHEN I EMERGED FROM the pit, the lady stood a few feet away, glitching like an old film reel. The night had been long. I could only assume that her energy was nearly spent, all the effort to appear to me, to guide me in her tasks, to carry Bethany's slight remains to me. It had all consumed her. Our time was nearly up. She pointed, and I merely nodded. Back to the house I went, walking slowly, my feet shuffling in the wet grass, the first rays of the morning sun warming my back. I opened the door that led into the kitchen, secured it behind me, then made my way down the silent halls to the library once more.

My heart was heavy. My head hurt, a constant throb in my temples from lack of sleep, from a night of stress, fear, and sadness, but behind it all, building ever so gently, was relief and a wave of gratitude that I had never felt before. The enormity of this night was not lost on me. Set aside the proof of the supernatural that I would carry with me from this day forward, but the lesson learned here tonight would never leave me. To be able to serve another in this manner, to release a soul from a devastating burden, to help another find some sense of peace in their darkest hour; that, for me, had become the biggest lesson of the night.

My life had been shallow and superficial, at best. Sure, I had friends, a good mother, adequate home life with almost all the worldly goods I could want. Within reason, of course, we were not wealthy, but we were comfortable. But I had never once thought about another like I had tonight. I had never once considered the pain that someone else might be enduring, the story behind someone else's life, or the reasons that may be at the heart of their actions. I had only ever considered myself, in all things. How I felt, how someone had made me feel, or made me cry, or made me feel any emotion that I did not wish to feel, but how many times had I done the same with zero consideration for the other side?

My mother crossed my mind as I crossed the threshold into the library. My own mother, alone in the world, my father long since passed, and I never once thought about what she carried with her. The burden of raising me alone without a companion, without family support, with barely any friends to lean on. How many nights had I left her home alone to sit in silence while I went to parties, to malls, to picnics, to any number of things that I enjoyed even when she had asked me to stay with her? Her quiet requests every once in a while, to stay home with her, to have a movie night, pizza and popcorn on the couch, or to spend the day shopping with her and I had scoffed at her ideas, laughing as I shut the door in her face.

My heart ached as I sank down on the chaise,

my mind entirely consumed by these thoughts. How similar were my mother and my lady? How much grief did my mom carry with her? How much loneliness did she keep hidden from me? She had never dated again, never remarried. She worked, and she raised me. Her entire existence centered on my life and my needs. Are these things a child worries about? Normally, parents would never put such things on their child, but as I grew as any child grows, should we not become more astute, more observant of others' needs and feelings, even those of our parents?

A kinder child would. A more observant child would have seen it. I simply had not. I was selfish and self-centered, and I felt sick with despair. Now, I wanted my mom more than ever. I wanted to spend the day with her on the couch. I wanted to go to lunch with her, to go to the beach with her. I wanted to see her smile without those shadows in her eyes. I had always thought that I was a good person, a good daughter, but in these early rays of dawn, my shortcomings were painstakingly clear.

I lifted my head from my hands, blinking tears from my eyes as I left a cold touch on my shoulder. The lady was standing beside me. Her sunken gaze was no longer the flashing red of anger and ire. It had softened to a golden amber, a steady glow. She backed away as I looked at her, removing her bony hand. She stood in the doorway, hands clasped before her waist, almost the image of who she had once been, elegant, patient, dignified. There was yet one final task.

I knew what it would be already. The lady waited somewhere in this house to be freed. Her body still lingered decayed and imprisoned some place within these walls, waiting to be put at rest. Her face cleared as I watched. The faint glitches seemed to render her new with each re-appearance. Her skirts were less tattered, her hair appeared a little neater, her skin changing from gaunt and sunken to just a little more fleshed out and rosy. The lady in the doorway now appeared more human than skeletal. I could almost see the beauty she had once been.

Wiping the tears from my eyes, I rose from the couch, patting my pocket to be sure I had my phone with me still. The candle had melted down to a nub and these halls would be dark for much longer despite the rising sun outside. She began her graceful glide up the marble staircase, and I followed. I felt my lips curve up into a smile as I watched her. Even her movements seemed lighter as she led me up the stairs. Her skirts swayed from her hips, swishing quietly across each stair. I felt as if each of my actions this night were helping her remember who she had been, as if by my setting things right for her, would allow her to forgive herself for her role in the tragedy and become her full self once more.

She led me down the hallway on the second floor, past the girls' bedrooms, past the schoolroom, to the attic doorway that stood in the shadows at the very end. She passed through it. I smirked, realizing that was the first time I had actually witnessed her going through a wall or door before. I grasped the doorknob and turned it, not surprised to feel the icy coolness of it. Up the narrow stairs I went, seeing her waiting at the top. The attic was dark and cold, shadows crawled across every surface while only the faintest glimpses of sunlight fought its way inside through the smallest cracks and pinholes in the board covered windows.

We stood in a main room with a hall about six feet beyond us. The central chimney of the house stood to my right. A fireplace set into the wall next to me. An old rocking chair leaned brokenly before it, a tattered blanket draped across it. A bookcase sat beneath a window, strewn with brittle leaves and cobwebs. Several books still lie scattered on the shelves. On the opposite side of the room stood a dining table with two chairs. Several cabinets to store supplies were positioned just behind it.

She waited, observing me as I looked around, then, catching my gaze once more, she turned and glided into the dark hallway. I swallowed hard, pulled my phone from my pocket to tap the flashlight app, and followed her. Darkness always brought forth my fear, and this was no different. The lady no longer filled me with terror, but the shadows, and what I might find within them, did.

SHE DRIFTED INTO THE shadows, her gown rustling in the stillness of the attic. The air was thick, stagnant, and stifling. I could see the pinpricks of light penetrating the dark like stars in a pitch-black sky, flickering and twinkling in and out of existence as the lady and I passed by. I became hyper-aware of the house, of its sounds as I followed her. The whispers of the dry leaves as we passed, the muffled groaning of rusty pipes and warped boards expanding as they absorbed the rainwater from the storm. The house breathed around us, the labored raspy breaths of an old lady about to leave this world.

My heart thumped within my chest, pounding beneath my breast as I tried to maintain my breathing, trying to remain calm through this last task. The others had been most unpleasant, but this task was weighing the heaviest on my mind. Knowing all that she had been through, I simply ached for her. I grieved for her in a way that maybe no one had ever done. It was entirely possible that no one had ever known what happened to her, or to her children.

The journal detailed the unraveling of the household, the captivity both she and Jonathan had faced, regardless of it being self-imposed. Only the doctor had any knowledge of what happened here, but if he had told anyone, there was certainly no evidence of anyone having come to set the family to rest. The task had been waiting for me. For nearly a hundred years, the mystery of this lonely manor had been left for me to find. I found myself suddenly grateful that it had been me. This night taught me much about myself and about how cruel life can be. Both lessons that I desperately needed.

I looked up from my musings, realizing the lady had vanished beyond the door to my left. I took a breath and placed my hand on the icy doorknob, and turned it. The door creaked open slowly, sounding exactly like every bad horror movie sound effect I had ever watched. A cold chill danced up my spine, and I shuddered. She stood in the middle of the room, staring at something in the corner. A bulky shape sat low beneath the small windows set in the wall. Windows that looked out over the front lawn, watching the lonely expanse of road as it passed by.

I moved closer to inspect the shape, running the weak beam of the flashlight over it. My mouth gaped open slightly as I bent low to the wooden box. It was a hope chest, ornately carved with vines and delicate flowers. Dust covered the surface, a heavy layer of grime and cobwebs clung to it, reaching from the shadows beyond. They swayed as I knelt down in front of it, my motions disturbing the silken threads for the first time in decades. I ran a hand over the top, sweeping the layer of dust aside, coughing as it wafted into the air, directly into my lungs as I inhaled. The scent of rot and decay coated my tongue. My heart pounded like a bass drum against my ribcage.

I looked over at the lady glitching in front of the windows. Sunlight dotted her shape like a thousand diamonds glittering at the bottom of a murky lake, muted and dim but there, glinting and shifting beneath the ripples. She gazed at me, through me, into the chest and beyond it. I could feel her eyes on me but not settling there. I knew she was staring past me, far into the past, into whatever lie within the chest. Cold dread settled in my gut.

Was this her grave? Her final resting place? Had the lady entombed herself inside this wooden box?

The irony was not lost on me as I looked from her back to the chest. A hope chest. A once traditional item given to daughters as they married, full of their hopes for the future to come. Bed linens, handmade blankets and gowns, intimates and delicates meant for the eyes of her husband, and tiny knitted blankets and satin baptism gowns for the babies to come. Some held fine china and silver, books and jewels, family heirlooms and other such items all meant to start the lady out on a fine path in life. *Was this chest hers? Or had it belonged to the nanny?*

I set my cell phone on the floor and lifted the latch on the front, unlocking the chest with a simple flick of the wrist. The dainty lock simply hooked into the loop when the box lid closed, hanging from above on a ring, allowing free movement of the curved metal. The hook slid right back into the loop below before I could lift the lid, so I moved it once more, this time holding my thumb against it as I began to lift the lid.

A foul odor assaulted my nose as the lid rose. Dry and brittle death drifted from the blackness within, assaulting me like a silent scream of release and relief and agony. The wood groaned open; the hinges protesting as I pushed the heavy lid fully open. My eyes only saw shadows. Dust swirled in the low light as I reached for my phone. A sigh emanated from behind me. The lady was close to me now, just behind my shoulder. I could feel the cold seeping into my back, my shoulders, and my arms as she hovered there waiting.

Phone in hand, I held it above the chest, tears already glazing my eyes over, knowing what I would see. Blinking rapidly, I cleared my vision, let the tears fall where they may and looked inside. The lady moaned behind me, a hideous sound of such sorrow that I gasped when it reached my ears. A deep sobbing wail that could only come from the deepest part of the human soul. It was endless in my mind as we both gazed upon what remained. A chill lodged itself in the base of my spine as her cry filled the room. It was a sound that I knew would haunt my nightmares from this day forth.

Her body lay inside, curled on one side, the tatters of her filthy gown surrounded the decaying remains of skin and bone. The thinnest of flesh that remained was pulled taut across her skeletal face; mouth open in what may have been her final scream. The expression was awful, terror etched across the furrows in the brow, the wide-eyed look the face still held. The stifling heat of the attic must have helped preserve her corpse as she lay inside, decade after decade, rotting inside her chosen tomb.

I looked from the head to the arms, to the hands frozen claw like at her sides, to the long nails that appeared shredded and broken and one bent almost the whole way back. I looked closer, shining the light on the other hand. The nails were the same. A black substance lined the nails and covered the fingers. Blood, I realized as I stared. Old, dried layers of blood from the cuts and scrapes on her hands. *But why? If she had entombed herself here, why would her fingers be so wounded?*

Shifting the light upwards, I gazed at the inside of the lid and my heart shattered again that night, falling to pieces inside my chest. I did not need a journal to understand. Clarity ran through me in an instant. Deep gouges marred the underside of the lid. Scratches in the wood, thin slivers still lifted from where the lady had scratched and pounded and pushed. Something shimmered dimly in the light, and I looked closer. One of her fingernails was still embedded in the wood of the makeshift coffin.

The cold left me suddenly, and I glanced up. The lady had moved to the foot of the chest and just stood there, looking down towards the bony remains of her legs and feet. Something pale stuck out from the lace layers of her skirt. I shifted to the end of the chest, still kneeling on the floor, and reached for it. A heavy parchment envelope met my searching fingers, and I pulled it free from the body.

Opening it with my cell phone propped beside me, I pulled three brittle pages free and began to read the final words the lady had left for me.

CHAPTER TEN

Oak Helm Manor–March 30, 1921

I'VE GROWN WEARY OF this existence. My body is weak and broken, as is my mind. I no longer care for the day, time or season. The house is black, pitch black at all hours, like the ruins of my heart. I will be dead soon. My flesh purples with bruises and sores. My hair falls to the floor in dry matted clumps as I pace the halls. My bones creak and rub against one another, worn down to the sinew that binds them. My dresses fall from my wasted body. Nothing left but bone to hold them. I care naught. I have covered the mirrors, the windows, and the doors. I see no reflection of what I was once, what I now am. I see nothing at all anymore except the faces of the dead. I hear their screams every time I close my eyes.

My pacing has taken me to the attic rooms. Here in the skeletal framework of the manor, I have found some semblance of peace. Here, the screams do not reach me as loudly. Here, in HER rooms, in the chambers where HE claimed her, I found the last remaining thing that was truly mine. The Hope Chest that was meant to carry me through a long married life, through days of happiness and joy, through long winter nights, and lonely days at home, through the birth of my children and holidays in our home.

The things are long gone. The blankets, the quilts, the christening gowns, the silver, and the jewelry, all those trinkets that were meant to speak of status and wealth, those things that were proper for a lady such as I, or rather, things that were proper for the lady I was groomed to be but am no longer. The chest had been emptied by my own hand upon arriving at the manor. They wait unused in the rooms below, stored in closets and cabinets and wardrobes, wasting away from neglect, much like their owner. Something else fills the chest now.

The chest of cedar that my father built with his own hands. Every nail placed by his strength, every carving chiseled with care, elaborate and unique and pleasing to my eye. All things that I adored in nature had been wrought into the sides and the top of this most extravagant gift. The ivy that clung to the sides of my childhood home. The delicate roses that mother doted upon. Images of the bluejay, the cardinal, and the squirrel, all can be found within the carvings stretched across the wood. A tree stands proudly on the rear side, all things branching out from it, up and over and around the chest. Swirls of life and beauty and creation all carved into this box for me to carry into a new life. A piece of my home to bring to the next. Now, it will carry me to my death.

Tears fail me as I write, even though my chest aches from the sobs that will not let go. The pain wracks my body; I shake with every breath. But my eyes do not glaze over with the tears of release. There are none left. I have not eaten more in days; I do not know when I last drank. This is my last act, these words so shakily scrawled upon this page, my final farewell, if anyone should find it. I doubt anyone will. There is no one left to care. These pages will follow me now to my chosen place of rest, the only solace I have found in recent days. The chest will keep me as I rest, from this life to the next, the chest and these words are all that I remain of the woman I was meant to be.

It is there that I now spend my hours, no longer pacing the halls like a wraith from beyond. I come here to the furthest attic room and climb into my chest. A single board props the lid scant inches open while I sink into its cold depths, closing my eyes to drift away for hours in this silent abyss. The screaming is not so loud here. I cannot see their faces here. Only muted quiet black ripples of memories of what once was. It is here that I think I shall die. Most fitting, I should *think, though I suppose the word I should use is irony. To die in the very thing meant to symbolize hope and new life. To waste away inside the only thing left that feels like home.*

If anyone finds this letter, then you have found my remains. Somewhere in this house lies my diary, a most tragic account of all that has happened in this place. My story is there. All you will need to know, if you wish to know. I have no final request, no last word or will or testament. If you find what is left, do what you will. There is no apology I can again utter, no forgiveness that I can seek, there is no way to make amends for the grief that has been wrought, for the madness that consumed me, for the tragedy that befell us all here in Oak Helm.

If you care, if you must act, then simply place me in the garden with my daughters, beneath the rose bushes from my mother. Let me rest there with my children. If you wish to help what remains find peace once again. I do not ask this as a request. I do not deserve such. I deserve to rot here in this box, within this house of misery and darkness. I do not deserve any kindness. I deserve to suffer in purgatory for eons before my soul descends to hell for my eternal punishment. It is what we all deserve, all except the children, the only innocents here.

It is time. I must go. Empty words written to no one, my own scornful laugh that bursts from my mouth sounds foreign and strange. It is done, enough of this lingering over pen and parchment. There is nothing left to explain. I shall remain here, wasting away until I die. It is all I deserve.

BY THE TIME MY eyes finished reading the shaky words, tears were falling in my lap, wetting my hands. The pain in my chest gripped me in such grief and sorrow that I wanted to scream it out for all to hear, but could not take in enough breath to do so. The sobs in my throat blocked any attempt. The lump of sadness and anger was too much to get around. So much pain has been wrought here. I let the tears come as I gazed upon the wretched soul in the box in front of me. I knew I would move her to the garden. She was my final task.

I shifted up onto my knees, gazing into the box at the wasted skeletal figure. Knowing what I now understood, her story was so much more tragic. Yes, her words said she put herself here to die, to waste away in the only familiar thing she had left, but I knew in my gut that something more had happened. The lady had become trapped here while she slept. Perhaps the board fell, maybe an errant kick of her leg or the flailing of an arm as she tried to escape her nightmares. Something made the lid fall and lock. The faulty board still lay next to the box, covered in dust.

The lady did not just quietly die. She suffocated, trapped and screaming in the dark. The proof was all there gouged into the lid, the scratches, the broken nails, the frozen rictus of her face, the terror etched upon her visage. She had died alone and terrified, a final act of tragedy, her fate more horrible than the one she had imagined.

I cried myself out, kneeling next to the makeshift coffin. I had not known her, but yet through her diary and her words and this shared night; I felt as if I did. I could feel her hovering in the shadows, calm and aloof, expressionless as I cried for her and for her family. Long moments passed while I settled myself and finally stood.

I turned to the shadow and spoke to her, seeing those red flickers of her haunted eyes piercing the darkness as she waited.

"I'll carry you to the garden. You will be with your daughters now. It is the least that I can do." I said to her softly, my voice barely a whisper in the thick silence of the manor.

"You can rest now. I'll finish this task."

She approached me; her tattered skirts rustling as she moved. She only gazed at me for a long moment, those eyes flaring like burning embers, then gave a single nod. She turned to her body; her head tilted down, looking at her corpse much like I had done moments before. I saw her presence glitch and fade, glitch, and fade, then settle. She turned to me, whole and flesh, for a brief moment, a radiant smile on a pale face. Eyes restored and sparkling. Her cheeks were pink and full. Her hair shining and properly fixed in a French braid. A single word reached my ears like a sigh on the wind rather than verbal utterance and she was gone.

"Thank you."

IN THE GARDEN, I said a brief prayer over the fresh grave. The lady could rest now, with her daughters beside her, in her beloved garden. There was not much left to say, not after the long night spent grieving with her and for her. I was utterly drained and exhausted, but somehow felt lighter than I had in years. The evening spent in fear and later, re-living such a tragedy with the lady of the manor, my own problems had all but disappeared.

I only knew that I wanted my mom. I had a lot to make up for and I looked forward to it. I brushed my hands off on my already filthy shorts and turned to go inside. The storm had relented, and the sun was climbing high in the sky, glittering off the windows and rain-slicked leaves and ivy. As weathered as it was, the manor was still beautiful. I smiled as I looked at it, nodding once as if to say, "you can rest now, too." The manor had protected the lady all this time, had kept her secrets and kept her safe from prying eyes, until she decided it was time to show herself, time for her to seek her peace, to set things right.

I pulled the rear door open and went inside, making sure to lock the door behind me as I went. Back through the house I went, cleaning up all traces of my night there, locking all the doors, tossing the remnants of my soup and tea from the night before. An idle thought entered my mind, and I slowly climbed the stairs to the attic one last time.

In the dark room under the back eaves, I knelt once more in front of the hope chest and carefully retrieved the letter from its depths. I sat with it for a long time, reading it again, trying to decide what to do next. Finally, I stood, decision made. I clutched the letter to my chest and turned away, making my way downstairs to the library again. There, I slid the letter inside the journal, and slid that into my bag. My phone chose that moment to ding as a text came through from my mom. Then several more.

"Worked the late shift. Home now. Are you okay? Where are you?"

I smiled and typed a quick message, then tapped the 'share location' button

"Long story. Battery almost gone. Sent you my location." I replied, waiting to make sure the message sent.

The ding sounded again with her immediate response.

"on my way."

"C U Soon. Love u." I texted back then typed again.

"Movie night? My treat?"

"sounds great."

I smiled when I saw her response, then slid my cell into my pocket; I slipped my bag over my shoulder and took one last look around the manor. It really was beautiful. But even more beautiful was the lesson I had learned here this night. The realizations that I had about my life, my mother, and her story, and how much I wanted to be a better daughter to her. A movie night was a small step, but a good one. There would be many more to come. I was fully committed to the vow I made here tonight. My mother deserved so much more than she had been given.

I left the house, the journal safe in my bag, knowing that one day I would tell the story of this lady in the manor, so she could live on in the memory of others, so she would not be forgotten and maybe I would tell my story too. I smiled as the sunlight hit my back as I walked down the path to the road to wait for my mom. The manor watched me leave, keeping its shadows and its secrets buried within.

ABOUT CANDACE NOLA

CANDACE NOLA IS A multiple award-winning author, editor, and publisher. She writes poetry, horror, dark fantasy, and extreme horror content. Books include Breach, Beyond the Breach, Hank Flynn, Bishop, Earth vs The Lava Spiders, The Unicorn Killer, Unmasked, The Vet, and Desperate Wishes. Her short stories can be found in The Baker's Dozen anthology, Secondhand Creeps, American Cannibal, Just A Girl, The Horror Collection: Lost Edition, and Exactly the Wrong Things, and many more.

Beyond the Breach, won the "Novel of the Year" and her Debut Novel, Breach, was nominated for "Debut Novel of the Year", for the 2021 Horror Authors Guild awards. She is the publisher and editor of the 2022

Splatterpunk Award Winning Anthology "Uncomfortably Dark Presents: The Baker's Dozen." She also won the 2023 Splatterpunk Award for anthology of the year for "Camp Slasher Lake, Vol. 1", with co-editor D.W. Hitz, published by Fedowar Press.

She is the creator of Uncomfortably Dark Horror, which focuses primarily on promoting indie horror authors and small presses with weekly book reviews, interviews, and special features. Uncomfortably Dark Horror stands behind its mission to "bring you the best in horror, one uncomfortably dark page at a time."

Find her on Twitter, Instagram, TikTok and Facebook and the website, UncomfortablyDark.com. Sign up for her Patreon for exclusive content, free stories, and more.

Website: www.uncomfortablydark.com

ALSO BY CANDACE NOLA

Earth vs The Lava Spiders

Bishop: Man Vs Monster

The Unicorn Killer

Sirens & Seaweed

The Vet

Venus

Desperate Wishes

Zippers

Zombie Ducks

<u>ANTHOLOGIES</u>

Uncomfortably Dark presents The Baker's Dozen-2021 Dark Dozen anthology & the 2022 Splatterpunk award-winning extreme horror anthology. Published by Uncomfortably Dark.

Uncomfortably Dark presents Trapped-2022 Dark Dozen anthology that explores themes of horror focused on being trapped in an unspeakable situation. Published by Uncomfortably Dark.

The Generator-quad collaboration anthology featuring Candace Nola, Eric Butler, M Ennenbach, and Nikolas P. Robinson. Published by Uncomfortably Dark.

Exactly The Wrong Things-Triple collaboration extreme horror chapbook with Joseph Monks and Franklin Wales. This is the authors' tribute to Ed Lee, Jack Ketchum, and Richard Laymon. "THE BEST PUPPET SHOW IN TOWN".

www.ingramcontent.com/pod-product-compliance
Lightning Source LLC
Chambersburg PA
CBHW061547310726
48972CB00008B/2643